Harold W. (Harold Wellman) Fairbanks

Stories of our Mother Earth

Harold W. (Harold Wellman) Fairbanks

Stories of our Mother Earth

ISBN/EAN: 9783744750264

Printed in Europe, USA, Canada, Australia, Japan

Cover: Foto ©Andreas Hilbeck / pixelio.de

More available books at **www.hansebooks.com**

WESTERN SERIES OF READERS — VOL. VI

Stories of Our Mother Earth

BY

HAROLD W. FAIRBANKS, PH. D.

SAN FRANCISCO

THE WHITAKER & RAY COMPANY

(INCORPORATED)

1899

INTRODUCTION.

NATURE study is deservedly attracting more and more attention in the schools, but the most of the aids for teachers and pupils have been limited to a presentation of organic nature, while the wide and fully as important field of inorganic nature has been very much neglected. With the hope of supplying, to some extent, the existing lack, this little book is presented for the use of grammar-grade pupils.

It has been the opinion of some educators that children are not as quickly or as easily interested in rocks, minerals, and the processes which are changing the surface of the earth, as in plants and animals. I believe, however, that where the experiment has been well tried, all phases of nature with which the child comes in contact, have been found to be equally interesting and instructive.

It is undoubtedly true that the study of specimens by themselves is largely devoid of interest. Children want to know the relation existing between things in the world about them. I am thoroughly convinced also that they are capable of understanding many of the processes involved in the shaping of the earth, but because of the idea that the subject is too difficult, or from lack of proper familiarity with nature on the part of the teacher, these inorganic nature studies are more often neglected.

The majority of children leave school at, or before, the completion of the grammar grades, and for these the great realm of inorganic nature has too often no meaning. We must reach these and give them at least some correct ideas of the origin and meaning of the common things about them.

In mountainous regions especially, where mining is often such an important industry, and physical nature seems to work more energetically, it is particularly desirable that the children should go out from school with some living knowledge of their surroundings. They should know something of those aspects of nature with which they have to deal their whole lives.

I do not wish to unduly emphasize the economic aspect of education at the expense of the so-called cultural, but I do maintain that the education of the child should bear some relation to his life's surroundings, and if, as is the case with nature studies, this education is cultural as well as economic, then so much the better. Those who pass their lives in the mountains with the rocks and minerals all about them, and the processes of disintegration, erosion, etc., actively at work, should be able, on leaving school, to interpret the more simple of these phenomena in a rational manner.

Nature study from books cannot be a success. Books should only direct to nature herself. Neither should nature study be an addition to already crowded courses but should supplant, especially in geography, much which is still too often taught irrationally and mechanically.

It has been my purpose in the preparation of the following chapters to present in a simple manner, some elementary conceptions in geology, mineralogy, and physical geography. While the different topics are illustrated by examples from the Pacific Coast, yet the most of them are of such a nature as to be applicable to any section of the country.

The Pacific Coast is particularly rich in illustrative material for the study of inorganic nature, but up to the present time little of this material has been put in such shape as to be available for the use of schools.

If the subjects presented here should prove helpful, even in a small degree, to teachers and pupils, and arouse in them a desire to know more of the processes of nature going on all about, the purpose of the book will have been accomplished.

HAROLD W. FAIRBANKS,
Berkeley, California.

May 15, 1899.

CONTENTS.

ILLUSTRATIONS.

THIS HOME OF OURS.

THE earth is our home. Ever since we can remember we have been living upon it, and moving about here and there. We have slowly become acquainted with some of its nooks and corners, but our rambles still bring us to many things which we do not understand.

As we climb the hills, or follow the rippling streams, or wander along the beach, we feel that this is a very pleasant place in which to live. For some of us the growing plants and flowers are the most attractive. Some like best to watch the strange behavior of the little animals and insects, while others think the smooth and brightly colored pebbles are of the greatest interest.

As we grow older, the world seems to widen out

REFERENCE TOPICS.

Interesting things right about us.

The changing earth.

We cannot combat Nature, we must take advantage of her ways.

Value of knowing how Nature works.

11

faster than we can explore it. We travel farther, and catch glimpses of a great range of snowy mountains, at the foot of which are broad fertile valleys, and beyond them the shining Pacific Ocean.

As we have a chance to examine this country closer, we find new things. The streams from the mountains are led out over the valleys, and keep them moist through the long summers, so that almost everything people need grows here.

In the mountains there are deep cañons through which, in the late spring, flow dashing streams of muddy water. In the fall they are quiet and clear, and we can count the pebbles over which they ripple. In some places they plunge over great walls of rock, and in others they run quietly under drooping willows.

High on the mountains there are no trees; only bare rocks and snow-banks. From a tall peak, we can see over the range to a very different region beyond. In that direction there are no green fields, no houses, nothing but a stretch of parched ground, for on that side of the mountains it seldom rains, and there are few running streams.

If we turn our footsteps to the ocean, we see in some places long ridges running out into the water. Where the waves have washed off the soil from these ridges there are jagged rocks, perilous places for the ships.

Behind the cliffs we see the bays, where the broad valleys come down to the ocean. The rivers wind sluggishly through these valleys, as though they did not know which way to go.

We enjoy seeing all these things, and by and by we begin to wonder about them, and to ask questions. The world becomes to us something more than a mere playground made for our especial benefit.

We begin to realize how large the world is, and how many things it contains which we shall have to study to understand. We see that life itself depends upon these things. If it were not for the great oceans from which the breezes carry moisture to the mountain tops, there to be condensed into rain, and water the thirsty land, no plants or animals could live, and our homes would become a parched desert.

We see that in choosing our homes we cannot go where we please, for we cannot grow our food in the desert, or upon the rugged mountains. We must choose the fertile valleys, if we would be farmers. We must leave the valleys and seek the mountains, if we would be miners.

Great cities do not grow up at any point. They are located in the protected harbor, behind the rocky headland, where the river and the valley meet the ocean, where the ships can come and take the produce. Manufactories must be built where dashing streams roaring among the bowlders, or pouring in cascades over the rocky cliffs, furnish the necessary power for running machinery.

It is clear then, that *our* lives, as well as the lives of the animals and plants, depend upon the oceans, the position of the mountain ranges, and the direction of the winds.

We question the mountains, and the rivers, and the ocean. We wonder if they have always been where they are now. The mountains look so firm and solid it seems as if they must always have stood where they do now. But some day we find shells upon a high ridge far from the ocean. This puzzles us, for these shells must have lived in the ocean once.

We finally come to the conclusion that before we can know all about the plants; why one kind grows on the hillside, another by the brook; why the animals are distributed as we find them; why cities grow up as they do; and why in one part of the country people till the ground, and in another part dig deep for the minerals, we must know a little more about the foundations of our home.

We must know how the rocks and the soil were made, how the mountains grew, and why the rivers run as they do. We must understand how Nature is shaping the earth about us.

In order to do this, we shall study what the rain and the frost are doing upon the mountain tops. We shall trace the river's course, and find where the mud which it carries to the ocean comes from. We shall try to understand how this mud is spread over the floor of the ocean, and what the waves are doing as they continually beat against the land.

We shall go beneath the rich soil upon which our grain grows, and find out what is going on within the earth. We shall want to know about many things which are dug from the earth,—how the coal was formed, and where the petroleum comes from. The gold, quicksilver, borax, and salt, will also interest us.

Nature has many forces at work, some great and some small. They have worked a long time getting this home of ours ready for us. If we can understand how Nature works, our home will be more dear to us, and we shall be happier.

BLACKBOARD WORDS.

Sluggishly (slŭg'gĭsh-ly) **realize** (rē'al-īz), **manufactories** (măn'ū-făk'tō-rĭz).

Parched = very dry.
Jagged = having rough sharp points.
Cascade = a small waterfall.
Foundation = that on which anything stands.
Perilous = full of danger.
Till = to cultivate.

SURFACE OF A RECENT LAVA FLOW IN MONO COUNTY, CAL.

THE ROCK FLOOR.

ELOW the loose earth upon which we walk there is a rock floor. This floor forms the crust of the globe, and stretches all around it. It is what makes the globe solid and firm.

When the rock floor was formed, a long time ago, it was very rough and uneven. Nature covered a part of it with the great oceans. Over another part she spread a dark carpet of soil; but she has not yet succeeded in covering the tops of the mountains.

Along the ocean cliffs the waves have washed away the carpet of soil, and we can see how rough and hard the floor is. We can also see the rock in the bottoms of all the little gulches in the hills; but in the valleys the floor is hidden very deeply.

How would the world look if there were no soil,

REFERENCE TOPICS.
The formation of the rock floor.
Lava.
The need of soil.
Different kinds of rock.
Where are minerals found?
The cooling globe.
Locate Mono Lake.

17

and everywhere we went we had to scramble over
the rough rocks? It may be that we can learn
something by a visit to a lava field where Nature
has not yet stretched her carpet of soil. Lava is a
part of the stone floor which was so hot at one
time that it melted and flowed up through cracks
in the crust of the earth.

Hundreds of years ago, near Mono Lake, in
Eastern California, some of this red-hot lava ran
out and spread over the surface, killing and burying all the plants, and the animals that could not
run fast enough to escape it.

It looks as if some giant had poured out there
a large kettle of thick pudding; but instead of
being good to eat, it was made of melted rock,
which, as it cooled, became so hard that a hammer
was needed to break it.

It is a long trip across the mountains to the lava-
field, but at last we come in sight of it,—an immense stretch of bare rock with green forests all
around.

We climb up the precipitous side of the lava,
and find, on reaching the top, an immense rough
plain of jagged rocks extending away in front as far
as we can see. There is not a tree nor bush to break
the desert-like character of the surface. As we climb
over the rough, sharp-edged rocks we can hardly
avoid tearing our clothes and cutting our hands.

It is the most lonesome place imaginable. There
are not even any little blades of grass growing out
of the cracks. All that we see are some patches of
gray moss, clinging here and there. Even the
birds and ground squirrels are absent, for there is
nothing here out of which they could build their
nests. Everything looks fresh and clean, as if it
had just come out of the shop.

In spite of care, we do sometimes slip and cut
our hands; and at last, tired of prying around, we
sit down on the edge of the lava and look at the
large pines growing in the soil of the valley
below.

We begin to wonder at the meaning of what we
have seen. It seems that the earth must be hot
inside, where this lava came from. If this is so,
then our whole world was hot once, even the outside, where the grasses and trees are growing. It
must have crusted over at last, just as our breakfast
mush cools on the outside first, or as the skim of
ice forms upon the pond during a cold night.

The rock upon which we sit certainly must have
been in the fire, for it looks just like the slag which
we have picked up about the furnaces where iron is
being melted. We try to imagine how the whole
country would look if it were covered with such
lava. We would find only hard rough rocks wherever we went. There would be precipices, deep

holes, caverns, and cracks, into which we would be in continual danger of falling.

It would rain as it does now, and the streams tumble over the rocks, as they hastened to the sea. The mountains would be white with snow in the winter time, but we would miss the spring, the green spring with its flowers, and the fall with its brightly tinted leaves. It would make no difference how much it rained; nothing could grow without soil.

The picture is such a dreary one that we stop thinking about it, for we could not live in a world of bare rocks and stones. Without the soil there could be no pretty little meadows, and without the plants which grow upon the meadows, no animals could live. It would be a dead world.

The whole world once looked just like our lava field, but that was so long ago that a great many changes have taken place. The stone floor which we now see is not all lava. Along the ocean beach, and in the beds of the rippling brooks, we see pebbles of many colors, telling us of the different kinds of rocks in the hard floor under us. There are so many that it would take a long time to learn all about them.

The stone which is used for the walls of buildings comes from this floor. It is dug from large holes in the ground called quarries. All the beautiful stones which are used for jewelry also come from the rock floor. They are rough, when first obtained, and have to be cut and polished.

Iron and copper are among the most useful of the minerals found in the rock floor, but we think the most of gold and silver. We should feel very awkward without many of these things which are dug out of the rocks, and we are glad that the soil does not cover them all up.

The mantle of soil furnishes the necessary things of life, and so makes it possible for us to live here; but the rock floor supplies not only many useful things, as we have seen, but, in the mountains, surrounds us with grand and beautiful scenery. It makes our lives more happy.

In the great plains of the Mississippi Valley, the rock floor is buried out of sight. The people living there do not know the pleasure of a home in the mountains, where the great rocks stand high in the air, and the rains and dashing streams have carved them into all sorts of grand and rugged cliffs.

In another lesson we shall see how the soil was formed, and at last covered up so much of the rock floor.

BLACKBOARD WORDS.

Precipice (prĕs'ĭ-pĭs), necessary (nĕs'ĕs-sā-ry), furnishes (fûr'nĭsh-ĕz), quarries (kwor'rĭz), imaginable (ĭm-ăj'ĭ-nȧ-ble), Mississippi (mĭs'ĭs-ĭp'ĭ).

Precipice = a steep place, a cliff.
Quarry = a place where stone is dug out of the earth.
Jagged = rough.
Crust = a hard covering.

HOW THE SOIL IS FORMED.

E learned from the lava field that there was a time, when our world was a good deal younger than it is now, when there was no soil upon its surface. The great oceans, and rivers, and bare rocks, were all there was to be seen.

Perhaps Dame Nature grew tired of such a barren world. However that may be, she at last covered up all but the roughest places with a smooth carpet. It was such slow work that I fear we would have become weary if we had been compelled to watch her. Look out upon the pretty valley and see how smooth and level she made the ground, and then turn toward the mountains where the great rocks rise to the sky, and you will see where she has not yet been able to spread the carpet of soil.

How did she do this

REFERENCE TOPICS.
The earth without soil.
How soil forms.
Work of animals in forming soil.
Residual soil.
Soil in valleys.
Work of the streams in removing soil.

THE SOIL COVERING THE ROCKS.

work, and where did she get the soil? It will help us to understand these things, if we look again, after many hundreds of years have passed, at the lava field near Mono Lake.

Generations of the great pines have grown up and died, when we again cross the mountains to the field of lava. How different everything looks. We have much trouble in finding the place.

The lava is no longer rough and bare, and only in a few places are there any rocks standing up from its surface. A soft, dark mantle of soil covers all the rest. Tall pines stand upon the soil, and send their roots down through it into the crevices of the lava below it.

In the side of a ravine we see what the soil is made of, and how it covers the lava. On the surface there is a dark layer of decaying leaves and stems, forming leaf-mold; and below it a dark, rich, clayey soil, with no fragments of the rock in it. Farther down it is almost a pure brownish clay, with only a few roots running here and there. This is the sub-soil. Below the subsoil, and near the bottom, there are fragments of the lava which crumble as we dig them out.

Under the subsoil lies the lava, which is soft and crumbling at the top; but in the bottom of the ravine, where the water has washed off the decayed lava, it is as hard as it was upon the surface so many years before.

We can also see in the sides of the ravine how the roots of the trees have grown downward into the cracks in the lava, and gradually shoved the pieces apart.

Year after year, ever since the lava first cooled, the rain and frost and air have been at work. For a long time they did not seem to accomplish much, but there are many things going on in the world which we cannot see.

The water ran into the cracks, and as it froze during the winter forced the masses of rock apart. The fragments finally crumbled and turned to a clay-like mass which formed a coating over the rocks.

Little by little, the seeds of different plants were carried to the lava field, either by the birds and squirrels, or borne upon the wind. Many of them, falling upon the crumbling rock where there was a little moisture, sent their tiny roots down into the cracks, and managed to live for a short time. When they died, their leaves and stems enriched the softened rock, and so, year by year, made the surface more fit for larger plants.

Trees grew up at last, and shaded the soil, so that the moisture did not dry out so fast, and when the trees died, they added their rotting trunks to the soil.

Then the ground squirrels came and burrowed in

the soft material, turning it over and over, bringing fragments of rock to the surface, where the frost made them crumble into still smaller pieces.

Many other animals made their homes in this gathering soil. Among them were the earthworms, which we see stretched upon the ground after a rain. They are stirring the soil all the time, and loosening it up so that the air can get into it.

The ants also are doing their part, as they tunnel through the earth, and bring the little particles to the surface. There are, in addition, some very small animals, which we can see only when they are placed under the microscope. They are called bacteria. Every handful of earth contains thousands of them. They are very necessary in fitting the soil so that the roots of plants can make use of it.

The soil which forms over the rock floor in this way is called residual soil. The brooks are washing away particles all the time, and this soil is what is left.

The soil in the valleys is formed in a different way. The tiny particles of sand and clay of which it is composed have, in many cases, been borne miles by the rivers, and ocean currents. All of the rock floor which we see in the mountains is softening and crumbling upon the surface just as the lava-bed did.

The raindrops wash the particles from the mountain slopes into the brooks, and they in turn carry them to the rivers. The latter leave them at last either in the marshes near their mouths, or bear them out to the ocean.

This is what the Sacramento River is doing year after year, as it pours its muddy flood through San Francisco Bay into the Pacific Ocean.

We will dip up a glassful of the dirty yellow water, and see what happens when it becomes quiet. In a few hours the water is clear, while upon the bottom of the glass is a thin layer of mud.

Each spring the Sacramento overflows its banks, and covers the lowlands. When the river becomes smaller and the water runs off the meadows, there is left everywhere a thin layer of mud. In this way the soil of the level bottom lands has been formed. Grasses grow upon it, and animals burrow in it, finally leaving it dark and rich.

We have already seen how necessary the soil is to our existence. Plants cannot grow without it, and without the plants there could be no animals.

We have also seen that it takes Nature many years to cover the bare rocks with this rich carpet. These things should make us careful when we plough and dig in it, that we do not leave it so the rains can carry it away. We should not permit the grasses and trees upon the hills to be killed, for their roots hold the soil. The soil in turn holds the moisture.

In the mountains of the desert there are few plants, and the soil is washed away as fast as it is formed, leaving the rocks almost bare.

BLACKBOARD WORDS.

Lava (lä′vä), **moisture** (mois′tur), **enriched** (ĕn-rĭcht′), **burrow** (bur′ro), **plough** (plou).

Lava = melted rock from a volcano.
Generation = those living at one period.
Ravine = a deep, narrow hollow worn out by running water.
Subsoil = the soil beneath the surface soil.
Marsh = soft, wet ground.
Burrow = to dig a hole in the ground.

WHAT IS LEFT OF A MOUNTAIN.

A HANDFUL OF SAND.

HAVE here a handful of clean, white sand, scraped up from the beach. It is the sand which the children so delight to play in, and which never soils their clothes.

It is the same kind of sand that they use to make mountains and hills in their geography studies.

Sand is not only nice to play in, but it is useful in many ways. Glass is made of it, and the plasterer mixes it with lime to form the mortar with which he lays the bricks, and plasters the walls of our houses.

What is the history of the little grains which the winds blow in our faces, and the waves wash up and down the beach?

Examine these grains with a pocket microscope and you will see that they are clear like glass and quite smooth. They have

REFERENCE TOPICS.
Origin of sand.
Composition of granite.
Crumbling of granite.
How the sand reached the ocean.
Sorting the components of the crumbling granite.

31

been thrown about by the waves, and rubbed upon each other, until all the sharp points are gone.

We will call them quartz grains and the sand, quartz sand.

Very long ago these grains of sand formed a part of a granite mountain. The mountain was high and rugged and stood upon the border of what is now one of the deserts of Southern California.

Now the mountain is nearly gone, and the little grains of which it was composed are scattered far and wide.

The picture before us shows a low hill in the desert. It is the heart of the old mountain, and is all that is left of it. How beautifully it tells the story of what Nature is always doing. She is tearing the rocks down in one place, and building them up again in another.

One lone granite pillar stands in the center of the hill. Lying about on all sides are the great blocks of granite which have broken off and tumbled down the sides of the hill.

These blocks are still hard, and if you should hit them with a heavy hammer they would not break. Those farthest from the hill, which have lain on the ground for a long time, are crumbling to little grains, which will form a part of the desert sands.

Scrape up some of the sand, and look at it carefully. It consists mostly of grains of quartz like those upon the seashore, only they have sharp angles instead of being rounded. Among the quartz grains are some little black scales and particles of clay.

With a hammer you can soon crush a piece of the granite to sand. Nature did not go to work in that way. She is very quiet, and it takes her many years to make great changes.

Let us look at a piece of the granite, to see what it is made of, and then, perhaps, we can understand how it crumbles to sand.

The clear, glassy grains which you cannot scratch with a knife, are the quartz about which we have been talking.

The shining black mineral which you can dig out in thin scales with the point of a knife is called mica. You have all seen it in the windows of stoves. The mica is used there because it is not easily broken or affected by the heat.

You will notice also some grains of another mineral, which is nearly white, but not as clear as the quartz. This mineral has little faces, which reflect the light, and it can be scratched a little with the knife. It is called feldspar.

Now let us see, if we can, how Nature changes a piece of solid granite to sand.

When the mountain of granite stood where the hill does now, there were narrow cracks running all through it. They were just like those which can be seen in the granite in the picture, if you examine it closely.

The rains soaked into the cracks, and the roots of the bushes and trees penetrated them. As the roots grew larger, they pried the masses of granite apart, just as a man would do with a bar. The loose pieces finally rolled down the mountain side.

As we have seen, every piece of granite is composed of three different minerals,—the quartz, the feldspar, and the mica. As the sun shone upon the granite it made it warm, and each grain expanded a very little. At night, when it was cool, the grains contracted. In this way they became loosened, and after a long time slowly fell apart, forming sand.

This is Nature's way of tearing down a mountain. It is very slow, but if you could live long enough you could see how much she accomplishes.

The little brooks which used to run by the granite mountain had plenty to do. As the granite crumbled, the feldspar became soft, and turned to clay. The brooks picked up the particles of clay first, but they made themselves muddy in doing so. They could not get rid of the mud which the clay made, and so had to carry it to the ocean.

The water also washed the scales of mica along very easily. Look in some brook on a summer day, and you will see the shining scales of mica moving along on the bottom with the current. Perhaps the brook is carrying them from some mountain which is now being torn down. The most of the little scales will not stop until they reach the ocean.

It was not so easy to move the grains of quartz, but the brooks did it when the rains fell, and they rushed along more swiftly.

The clay and the mica scales were carried far out into the ocean, where the water was quiet, and then fell to the bottom.

The quartz grains were not carried out so far, and the waves piled them up on the beach. The waves never tired of playing with the sand. They turned the grains over and over, and ground them together, until they were perfectly smooth.

You see now how the ocean sorted the different minerals in the granite. It put the clay and mica scales in one place, and the quartz grains in another. The work is not always done so well, for along some ocean shores the clay and mica and quartz are all mixed together.

When the waves have done with the grains of sand, and thrown them up high on the beach, the wind takes a hand. It picks them up and whirls them through the air as it does the snowflakes.

What do you suppose will become of the granite pillar which is all that remains of the mountain about which we have been talking? It seems to defy the rains and the frost, but by and by it also will fall, and crumble to sand. Then there will be nothing left to tell of the mountain but a small mound of sand in the desert.

The forces of the weather never rest. They are tearing down all the mountains around us. Although the carpet of soil in which the trees and grasses grow protects the rocks in many places, yet they are crumbling and decaying in spite of it.

After a time the mountains will all disappear, if something does not lift them up again.

We love the wild rocks, and do not like to think of their being torn down; but we must be content, because their materials are necessary to make the soil.

BLACKBOARD WORDS.

Microscope (mī′krō-skōp), mica (mī′ka), feldspar (fĕld′-spär′), defy (dē-fī′), decay (dē-kā′).

Granite == a rock, composed of quartz, feldspar, and mica.

Quartz == a hard, glassy mineral.

Feldspar == a constituent of rocks. Clay is formed from feldspar.

Mica == a mineral separable into thin flexible plates.

Scale == a thin layer of any substance.

Mound == a little hill.

Pillar == an upright support; a column.

THE WORK OF THE WIND.

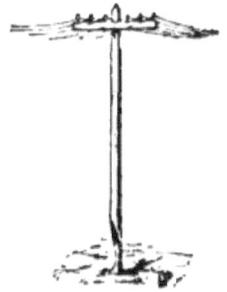

HERE are many different forces at work around us. The world is never free from them, although they go about their business so quietly we cease to notice them.

The frost, the raindrops, the river, and the ocean waves are all doing something toward leveling the surface of the earth.

The wind also has a share in the changes which are going on. It is different from the other forces, in that it builds up hills as well as causes them to be worn away.

When the trees are bending before the storm, and the great breakers are coming in from the ocean, we see what power the air has as it rushes along.

We realize still better what the wind can do if we try to face it. The grains of sand, and even small pebbles scattered

REFERENCE TOPICS.

Various ways in which the wind works.

Sand storms.

The effects of flying sand.

Sand-dunes.

37

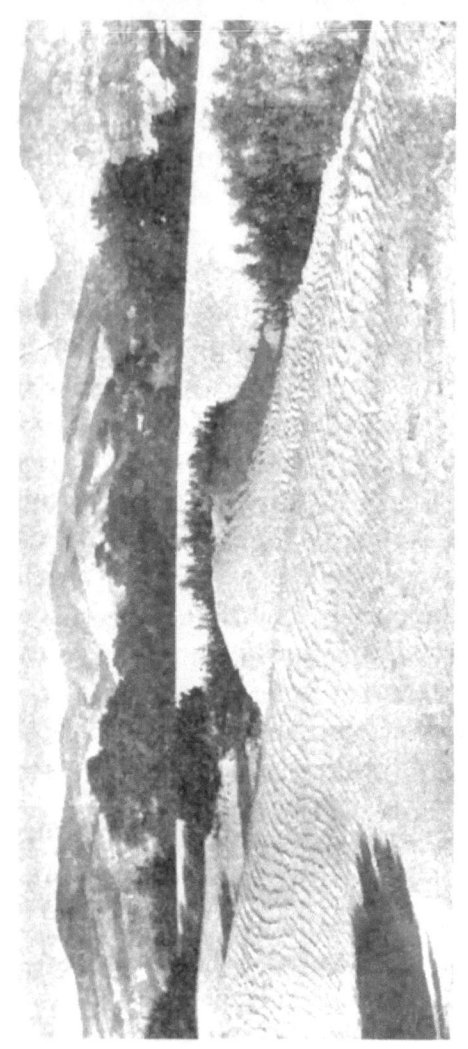

over the ground, are picked up by the wind and thrown in our faces with such force as to make the flesh tingle with pain.

The wind does work then. It uses the sand to grind down the bare mountains in the deserts. When it is through with the sand for a while, it piles it up into great hills, called dunes.

The most of us have seen the dust storms, when a "norther" is blowing. The sky is yellow, and the sun almost hidden by the flying dust and sand. It gets into the tightest houses, and settles on everything.

In the deserts the sand storms are furious things, for there is nothing to break the sweep of the wind. In the deserts of Arabia and Northern Africa, people are sometimes smothered and buried in the sand storms.

After feeling the powerful blows of the little grains upon one's face, it is not hard to understand how mountains can be worn away by them.

In the deserts the rocks have but little, if any, covering, and the winds blow much of the time. With the wind behind them, the little grains are forever chasing each other over the surface. If any rocks get in the way, they have to suffer. Each grain is a chisel in the grasp of the wind, and every time one strikes, it takes a very small bit of the rock away with it. The rocks are thus sculptured into all sorts of pinnacles and grooves.

The sand plays strange freaks sometimes. Along the railroad, in the Colorado Desert, it cuts into the telegraph poles until they are worn through.

The beautifully polished pebbles which are scattered over the desert owe their shining surfaces to the blows of thousands of grains of sand, which are always moving along the ground when the wind blows.

In some portions of the Colorado Desert the wind has piled the sand into great dunes. They do not stay in one place, as hills usually do, but move across the country in the direction in which the wind generally blows. They march in ranks, like an army, destroying everything in their path.

The dunes are formed in the same manner as snowdrifts, and are shaped exactly like them. The sand drifts upon the railroad tracks as the snow does in the winter in the mountains, so that trains are stopped until it can be shoveled off.

The work of the wind in forming dunes is most frequently to be seen along the ocean. For miles and miles the ocean waves break upon a cushion of sand. The rivers have brought some of the sand from the far mountains. Some of it the waves themselves have made, as they ceaselessly hammer the pebbles upon each other.

Each breaker lifts the grains of sand, whirls them around, and throws them up the sloping beach.

Some are left high and dry, above the reach of the succeeding waves. Then, as soon as they are dry, the wind takes them in charge. It rolls them over and over, or carries them bodily through the air, and finally piles them up in those great drifts, which we have called dunes.

As our picture shows, each dune is long and narrow, and looks exactly like a snowdrift, even to the little ripples upon its surface. The manner in which the dunes travel is as follows: the wind picks up the grains of sand on that side of the dune from which it blows, and carries them over the top. As soon as they reach a point which is protected from the wind, they are dropped. Thus they succeed each other, as the dune slowly moves inland from the beach.

Nothing can stop the march of the dunes. Bushes, trees, and green meadows are buried under the barren sand. The only way in which dunes can be held is to get bushes or grass to grow upon their surfaces. Then the wind can no longer get hold of the sand.

On some coasts, the sand-dunes have overwhelmed whole farms, and even villages. If a village stands in the way of the creeping dunes, the people have to leave. The houses are buried, and all traces of the village disappear for years. But, as the dunes continually move, the houses may be uncovered in time.

What a dreary sight the deserted village presents, with the broken houses, and dead trees still standing in front of them.

Our picture shows some beautiful dunes upon the edge of the Salinas River, in Monterey County. The river bottom is dry in the summer, and the winds have drifted the sand over the bushes and trees.

BLACKBOARD WORDS.

Realize (rē'al-īz), **tingle** (tĭn'g'l), **dune** (dūn), **sculpture** (skŭlp'tūr), **pinnacle** (pin'-na-k'l), **overwhelm** (ō'ver-hwĕlm').

"**Norther**" = a heavy wind from the north.

Chisel = a tool with a cutting edge on one end.

Overwhelm = to cover over completely.

Sculpture = to carve or cut.

Pinnacle = a high, sharp point.

A CURIOUS CALIFORNIA RIVER.

OME of our California rivers have strange ways. They do not act as rivers ordinarily do. They seem to flow bottom-side up. Ordinary rivers run upon the top of the ground and become larger toward their mouths.

These curious rivers are found in portions of California where the rainfall is light, and they have to run a long distance to reach the sea.

The Salinas River is one of them. As we study the map of California, this river appears to be one of the longest and most important streams in the Coast Ranges. If you should start out in the summer time to look for this river you would be disappointed. You can find the Salinas Valley easily enough, but where is the river?

There, where it ought to

> REFERENCE TOPICS.
>
> Characters of ordinary rivers.
> Behavior of rivers in dry regions.
> Salinas River.
> Effects of summer heat.
> How the sand preserves the water.

THE DRY BED OF THE SALINAS RIVER AS IT APPEARS IN THE SUMMER TIME.

be, is a winding channel of sand, reaching as far as you can see. High clay banks shut in the bed of sand, which is half a mile wide. It must be the river bottom, although there is apparently no water in it. Every few miles it is spanned by long iron bridges, so that it must be that water flows here sometimes.

What then, has become of the river? Its bed is so dry that the afternoon sea breezes which sweep up the valley and across its surface, blow the sand into great drifts.

The sand in the bed of this apparently dry river is very deep. If you should dig down a few feet it would become moist, and a little farther, you would meet water. Now you have found the river. How strange! The sand, which is usually at the bottom, is on the top. The river is actually flowing through the sand, instead of on the surface. Why does it do this? The reason is very simple.

During the long dry summers the hot sun dries up so much of the water that there is not enough to rise above the sand, which is piled deep in the bed of the river.

The sand is like a sponge, because it absorbs a large amount of water. As the little grains are not packed tightly together, there are little empty spaces about each one. Through these spaces the river slowly passes down its sloping bed to the sea.

In the winter the storms are frequently severe, and floods of water are brought by all the rivulets to the main river. Then the flood sweeps down the channel, washing down its banks until it forms a broad sandy bed.

Far away in the gulches are hidden the little springs which feed the river during the summer. The grasses and ferns shade them, while overhead bend the pines and oaks, and the hot sun cannot get at them.

Farther down the slopes, the springs unite in the rivulets which run more slowly, and are in many places open to the sun.

These little streams at last unite in the main river which, for a time, runs over a rocky bed between the hills.

Soon the banks become more open; the hills leave the river, and a broad valley takes their place. The river seems to hesitate about going farther, for there are no longer tall trees and overhanging banks to protect it from the rays of the greedy summer sun. With what intensity they beat down through the long days.

The river seems doomed, for it would all be gone long before reaching the sea if it had to flow over the hard rock floor which it had among the hills.

But the sand comes to the rescue. The little grains of sand, which the river has been trying for so many years to wash out of its bed and carry to the sea, now do the river a good turn. The sand was in the river's way, and blocked its channel, when it swept along so full and strong in the winter. Now the river is glad to accept its protection.

The sand has buried the rock floor all the rest of the way to the ocean. Gladly does the river creep in between the little grains, and hide itself from the sun. It looks a little selfish however, for now the thirsty cattle follow its bed for miles, hunting in vain for some water to drink. They are fortunate if they at last find a little spot where the sand is so shallow that the river has to come to the top. It peeps out for a few rods, and then disappears again in the sand.

How wise Nature seems in thus preserving the river, which would otherwise be entirely dried up by the summer heat. It furnishes water to the people who live along its banks, who would otherwise have trouble in getting it. Now all they have to do is to dig a hole in the sand of the river bed, and there they find plenty of pure, cool water.

Although the river flows upon the top of the sand for only a little time each year, yet the bridges are quite necessary. When the sand is full of water, it forms what is called quicksand. It is then very dangerous. A team will sink into it almost as quickly as into water, and it is very hard to get it out.

Where the sand is very deep, as in the deserts, it drinks up all the water that falls and never gives it back.   In our rivers the bedrock keeps the water near the surface.

As the days become cooler in the fall, the air does not take up so much of the water, and a little of it again comes to the top, and runs over the sand. It increases until the first heavy rains come, when the broad winding strip of sand becomes a muddy torrent.

Streams in South America which head in the high mountains, and flow across the deserts, have the same habit.   When the snows begin to melt on the distant mountains, the people go out to watch for the coming of the river.   When it does come running down over the dry sand they are happy, for without the water there would be no crops the coming year.

BLACKBOARD WORDS.

Hesitate (hĕz′ĭ-tāt), intensity (ĭn-tĕn′sĭ-ty), protection (prŏ-tĕk′-shŭn), preserving (prē-zĕrv′ing), irrigate (ĭr′rĭ-gāt).

Coast Ranges = a series of mountain ranges bordering the Pacific Coast of the United States.

Gulch = a ravine, or deep bed of a torrent.

Shallow = having little depth.

Irrigate = to moisten land by means of a stream made to flow over it.

THE STORY OF SAN FRANCISCO BAY.

NATURE has been a long time making California. She has put gold in one place, and silver in another. She has lifted up mountains, and torn them down again.

She has buried the Coast Ranges under the ocean, and then raised them up again as though she enjoyed the sport.

She has turned things upside down so many times that we are not quite sure she will not do it again. How strange it would be if we should wake up some morning and find San Francisco Bay dry land. Stranger things than that have happened here.

Can you picture to yourselves how San Francisco Bay would look if there were no water in it; if

REFERENCE TOPICS.
————
Former condition of San Francisco Bay.
Trace on the map the old course of the Sacramento River.
Submerged valley in Monterey Bay.
Bay filling up.
Location of cities.
Islands in the bay.

49

SAN FRANCISCO BAY.

the fertile valleys which surround it extended all over it?

There would be room for many farms, and quantities of vegetables could be raised. However, they might not find sale, for if there were no bay here, there would be no city of San Francisco. There would be no Golden Gate, with the ships sailing in and out past the lighthouses and the foghorns.

This is the way it really was many years ago. The land was much higher, and the Sacramento River flowed where the bay now is. Did the river empty into the ocean where the Golden Gate is? We will answer the question by asking if it could have flowed anywhere else, if some giant had built a great dam across the mouth of the bay?

There is, indeed, another way. It is through the Santa Clara Valley, past the city of San José. This broad valley is only slightly raised above the level of the ocean, and extends south to the Pajaro River, which flows into the bay of Monterey.

The Santa Clara Valley is so nearly level that, as you ride through it on the cars, it is hard to tell just where the highest point is. On the north, the streams flow into San Francisco Bay. On the south, they unite with the Pajaro River and so reach Monterey Bay.

You can see now that if the mouth of San Francisco Bay were dammed up, the Sacramento could easily flow south into Monterey Bay. What a strange sight it would be to see this large river flowing past Oakland and Alameda, and through the Santa Clara Valley, where the city of San José now stands.

You know from the geography the shape of Monterey Bay, and where the Pajaro and Salinas rivers flow into it. It has been discovered by soundings that there is a great valley extending east and west through the bay, but entirely buried by the ocean.

It is believed that when the land was higher, and Monterey Bay was dry land, that a large river flowed through this valley. You can easily guess what river it was. It was that which we call the Sacramento.

Then a time came when the coast sank, and all the lowlands along the shore were flooded. The sea, of course, broke through the Coast Range of mountains at the lowest point, which is the Golden Gate. After this happened, the Sacramento River did not have to flow away round by San José and Monterey to get into the ocean, but could go directly through the gap made in the hills between San Francisco and Sausalito.

While the bay region was dry land, several hills rose in the fertile valley. When the ocean broke in and flooded the land, the hills which were not entirely covered up, formed islands. One of these we call Goat Island, another Angel Island, and a third, Alcatraz Island. Those hills which were just covered by the water, formed reefs. The reefs did no harm to the canoes of the Indians, but when the great ships came some ran onto the rocks and were injured.

To make the Golden Gate more safe for ships to pass through, these rocks will have to be blown out.

The Sacramento River, and the smaller streams which flow into it, are continually at work trying to fill up the bay. They do this by the aid of the mud and sand, which the rains wash into their channels.

Many small arms of the bay are already so nearly filled that the bottom is exposed at low tide. The marshes back of the mud flats are high enough for a kind of grass to grow upon them.

The long wharves, which have been built out into the bay, break the currents of water which are carrying mud out into the ocean, and more of it settles to the bottom. In order to dig out this mud, which is settling all the time, machines called dredgers have been built. They scoop up the mud from the bottom, and so keep the water deep enough for the great ships.

Man is helping Nature fill up San Francisco Bay, and many years from now it will not be as large or as deep.

This is not all of the history of San Francisco Bay. Many other things have happened here. It was once so deeply buried beneath the ocean that only the tops of the Berkeley Hills, Mount Tamalpais, and the Santa Cruz Mountains, rose above the water.

The ocean extended up through the straits of Carquinez, past Vallejo and Benicia. The San Joaquin and Sacramento Valleys formed large, deep bays into which ships could have sailed if there had been any people to sail them.

Now that we know something of the story of San Francisco Bay, we may wonder why the great city which bears the same name was built here. Did you ever think that we cannot build a city anywhere that we want to? We have to take advantage of the way in which Nature has arranged the mountains, valleys, and bays.

If California had been discovered and settled at a time when San Francisco Bay was dry land, you may be sure that no great city would have been built here. The city would have grown up where there was a harbor for ships. It might have grown up on Monterey Bay.

Where a number of inland streams and valleys unite in a deep and protected bay, that is the place for a great city to be built. So you see why the largest city of the Pacific Coast has grown up on San Francisco Bay.

The bay has a narrow entrance, and is well protected from the storms. It is broad and deep, and its long arms reach out into the many valleys which converge toward it. Nature has destined it to be the centre of trade of a great region.

How much more interest the bay will have for us, now that we know something of its history.

BLACKBOARD WORDS.

Vegetable (vŏj′ĕ-ta-b′l), **Pajaro** (pä′-hä-rŏ), **Sausalito** (saw-sä-lee′to), **Alcatraz** (äl-kä-träz′), **Tamalpais** (ta-mal′pïs), **Vallejo** (val-lä′ho), **Benicia** (be-nish′e-a), **Salinas** (sä-lee′näs), **dredger** (drŏj′-er).

Submerged = under water.

Scoop = to shovel, or dip up with a ladle.

Sounding = ascertaining the depth of any part of the ocean.

Reefs = Rocks at or near the surface of the water.

Converge = to approach nearer together.

Destined = set apart for a use or purpose.

AN ANCIENT OYSTER BED.

NEAR the summit of the Coast Ranges, far from the ocean, I found an oyster shell. There it lay in the sandy soil, looking so old and worn, I could imagine that hundreds of years had passed since it saw the ocean.

Did some one carry it there, or did a bird bring it from the seashore? It hardly seemed possible, for there are none like it upon the beach. Besides, there are no birds living now which could carry a shell of such size.

The one which lay before me seemed a giant in comparison with those in the market, and is properly named *Ostrea titan*. The oyster which once lived in this shell would have made a whole meal. A half dozen of the common oysters would hardly make more than so many mouthfuls.

REFERENCE TOPICS.
A bed of fossil shells.
Where oysters live.
Picture of the ancient oyster bed.
A catastrophe.
Elevation of sea bottom.

If you had ordered some oysters in a restaurant, I think you would be astonished to see a waiter come in, carrying a single big oyster upon a platter. Just think of an oyster with a shell a foot and a half long. Such a big fellow would have to be carved like a piece of roast beef.

Many such oysters must have lived once upon a time, for on looking about near where I had found the first one, I discovered a whole bed of them. They were sticking out of a layer of hard sand, which extended along the top of a low hill.

Where the rain had washed the dirt away, other and smaller shells appeared. There were scallops and periwinkles, and clams which looked very much like those now living in the ocean.

The layer of sand and fossil shells looked just like an old sea beach; but how did it come here, high in the mountains? Oysters do not live in rivers or lakes. They are found only in the salt water.

The Coast Ranges must have been under the sea a long time ago. As the earth was raised the water ran off, and the place where the shore was at that time is now many miles from the ocean.

Suppose you try to form a picture in your mind of that old beach where the oysters lived in the clean, white sand.

There were not many things to disturb the peace

AN ANCIENT OYSTER BED ON THE COAST OF SOUTHERN CALIFORNIA.

and quiet of the great oysters, whose shells were so thick that no animal could bite them open. Besides, there were then no people living upon the earth. So that they were not troubled by picnic parties, or the men who hunt for oysters at low tide, in order to carry them off to market.

Many generations of the oysters lived there happily in the shallow water, among the islands where the Coast Ranges were to stand in the distant future.

The oysters had plenty to eat, and their shells grew so large and heavy that they could hardly open them. When they died, the waves buried them in the clean sand. The young oysters took their places, and in this way the bed of sand and shells became many feet thick.

The ocean tides rose and fell twice a day in those times, just as they do now. The oysters did not mind it. In fact, they rather enjoyed the little time during which the tide ran away and left them.

But one day something unlooked for happened. The tide went out farther than usual, and left the bed of oysters bare for a long time. After a few hours had passed, and the salt water had dried off from them, they became very thirsty. O, for a drink of the cool salt water. Why did the hot sun shine upon them so long? Why did not the tide come back?

Their shells gaped wider and wider; but alas, it was all in vain. In a little time they all died.

When it was too late the tide swept in again; not quietly as it had done so many times before, but with a rush of muddy, dashing waves. The water came in with such force that it did not stop until it had swept far over the land, uprooting the trees and washing away the soil.

The currents and waves washed mud and sand and rubbish from the land over the bed of oysters, and it was buried very deep.

The water kept rising, until it covered all of the islands, and there was no land in sight.

After ever so long a time had passed, the water began to go down, and the land where the islands had been, rose again above the water. The land continued to rise, and after a time the water all ran off. The islands became connected by dry land, and so were no longer islands.

This land which had been raised above the water was only bare rocks and mud and sand. It looked just as San Francisco Bay would look if the water were all drained off.

The winds and the birds brought seeds, and all kinds of plants sprang up where the sea used to be.

You may wonder what became of the bed of oysters. It was so completely buried that one would never suspect there had ever been one.

Something was raising the land higher all of the time, and by and by it began to look a little like our Coast Ranges. The rains which fell washed out little ravines, which finally grew to be cañons. The rains also worked upon the hills, and washed away into the cañons so much of the rocks and soil that the bed of oyster shells at last stuck out of the ground in plain sight.

This is the history of these rough and worn oyster shells. What fun it is to dig them out of the sand where they have been buried all these years.

BLACKBOARD WORDS.

Oyster (ois'ter), **Titan** (tī'tan), **gape** (gäp), **periwinkle** (pŏr'I-win'k'l).

Oyster = a marine mollusk, of the genus Ostrea.

Titan = pertaining to the Titans, of great size.

Fossil = remains of a plant or an animal found in stratified rock.

Tide = the rise and fall of the sea.

Scallop = a bivalve shell with radiating ribs.

Periwinkle = a small gastropod shell.

A RAINSTORM IN THE DESERT.

YOU have all heard of the deserts of Eastern California. They are formed of broad, sandy valleys, with mountains of almost bare rock, lying between them.

The high mountains, between these deserts and the coast, cut off the cool breezes, and during the long summer days the air becomes so hot that when it blows upon one's face it seems like the breath from an oven.

It is not the heat, however, that makes this region a desert. It is so barren because there is very little rain. One would think that the lizards and the rattlesnakes would have such a country all to themselves.

The desire for gold, however, draws men across the blistering sands to the far away mountains, and some of them are never heard of again.

Two prospectors once made their camp in a range of mountains in the Mojave Desert. They had been fortunate, and found a cool spring which no one but Indians had seen before. They built a cabin in the cañon near it, for they intended to stay there and hunt for gold.

The cañon extended away back into the mountains, and some time, water must have flowed in it, but now it was perfectly dry. As rains so seldom fell upon the mountains the prospectors felt quite safe.

During the middle of the hot days little columns of sand were caught up by the winds, and moved slowly across the sandy desert at the mouth of the cañon. Fleecy clouds also gathered about the tops of the mountains, but disappeared as night came on.

Months passed quietly in the cañon, but one day the clouds gathered heavier than usual. They grew quite black, and a few rumblings of thunder were heard.

The miners looked at the clouds so far away, and longed for their cool shadows, but after a time, as the sun continued to shine upon them, they forgot all about the clouds.

In the meantime something was happening in the dark clouds. They settled down upon the tops of the mountains, and a few drops began to fall. As these drops cooled the air, the clouds sent them down thicker and thicker. Finally a perfect flood was pouring from them upon the barren mountain slopes.

A CACTUS GARDEN IN THE COLORADO DESERT.

There was little soil to hold the falling drops, and they quickly gathered into rills. The rills ran over the ledges of rock and into the little ravines. They poured from all sides, for the clouds seemed to have broken and turned all of their moisture into raindrops at once.

The floods of water tumbled and roared into the gulches. They became larger each moment, as every side cañon added its share. The torrents were angry and muddy looking. They had picked up what little soil there was and all the loose fragments of rock, besides, there were trunks and branches of the few stunted trees which managed to live upon the mountains.

It was years since such a rain had fallen here, and a large amount of rubbish had accumulated. Many fragments had fallen from the cliffs into the cañons, and one might think that the water would have trouble getting over or around them.

On the contrary, it did not seem to be delayed at all. It picked up and carried along all but the very largest ones, apparently as easily as it did the bird's nest which had been torn from a bush.

In a short time all the torrents reached the main cañon. There they united and went thundering down toward the little cabin of the miners. The men had heard the sound of the coming waters, but did not know what it meant until a wall of water appeared sweeping around a bend in the cañon above them.

In an instant the men were out of the bed of the cañon, and climbing its sides. They were just in time to reach a point of safety as the foaming flood went thundering past.

At its front, huge bowlders, almost as large as their cabin went rolling over and over. The water was thick with mud and sand and bowlders.

The clouds had cleared away, and the rain stopped by the time the flood had reached the main cañon, and so the water went down almost as quickly as it had risen. After a few hours, there remained only a little stream of muddy water, hunting its way among the bowlders which dotted the bed of the cañon.

The miner's cabin had escaped the torrent, but just in front of it was a dirty channel, many feet wide. The willows by the spring had been swept away, and all was dirty and desolate.

What had become of the great mass of water and rubbish? It swept down to the mouth of the cañon, and there spreading out upon the sandy floor of the open desert, soon spent its force. Some of the bowlders were carried three miles out into the desert. The water did not stop there, but with the mud and sand, flowed fully ten miles before it sank into the dry sand.

This is the picture of what we generally call a cloudburst. When rains fall upon the mountains of the desert they often come in torrents of this kind. As there is so little soil, the water gathers and runs off very quickly.

In places where it rains more frequently, soil collects, and the grasses and trees which spring up keep it from washing away.

We can easily see that the desert mountains will finally be torn down by such cloudbursts. The mountain tops are cool, and at times change what little moisture there is in the air into raindrops. When the mountains have been worn away the springs will dry up, and the desert become more barren still.

BLACKBOARD WORDS.

Mojave (mō-hä́'vä), **fortunate** (fôr'tū-nāt), **condense** (kŏn-dĕns'), **column** (kol'ŭm), **accumulate** (ăk-kū'-mū-lāt), **moisture** (mois'tūr).

Prospector = one who hunts for minerals.

Gulch = a ravine; deep bed of a torrent when dry.

Stunted = dwarfed.

Rubbish = waste matter.

Cloudburst = a sudden, heavy rainstorm.

Condense = to change into another form by cold or pressure.

Moisture = that which makes damp or wet.

A FAR SPRING IN THE COAST RANGES.

THE STORY OF PETROLEUM.

HERE was a time very long ago when there were no Coast Ranges in California. The waves of the Pacific Ocean rippled in the sunlight, where the cities of San Francisco, Santa Barbara, and Los Angeles now stand. In this old ocean the hungry porpoise chased the little fishes, and many strange monsters swam to and fro.

Sometimes the sailor thinks that he catches sight of some of these long, snake-like monsters playing near his ship. No one believes him, yet he may be right, for we know by the bones which have been found that there were once such animals in the sea.

You have read of the whales, those great animals which are hunted for their oil; but did you ever think that the petroleum in our evening lamps also comes from the sea, from the

REFERENCE TOPICS.
Animals of the ocean.
Necessity of sunlight.
Bottom of the ocean.
Ooze.
Petroleum.
Tar, bitumen.
Bituminous rock.
Uses of petroleum.

bodies of very small animals which lived long ago? It is a strange story, and you may be interested in hearing it.

The world did not look then as it does now, though the ocean was filled with plants and animals swimming or floating in it just as at the present time. They did not know nor care that the bottom of the sea in which they lived was to be called California. All they wanted was sunlight, plenty to eat, and a great ocean in which to live.

In order to find out more about these little animals, and what became of them when they died, let us take an imaginary trip to the bottom of that old sea. We shall have to be dressed as divers are, with helmets on our heads, and heavy weights attached to our feet.

The bright sunlight follows us down many feet, as we sink through the clear water, but it gradually becomes dim, and, long before we reach the bottom, it is as dark as it is at midnight, when the stars are hidden by heavy clouds.

In the upper portion of this sea the water is full of animals and plants of every size, shape, and color. The fishes and their relations stare at us for an instant with their great round eyes, and then are gone. But the little animals, which are not much more than mouth and stomach, are not at all disturbed by our visit.

We see that each layer of water has its peculiar animals, just as each kind of bird has its own place in which to live, and build its nest. The bodies of the most of these animals are so small that, as they float before our eyes, they seem like so many particles of dust. A cupful of water would contain thousands of them.

As the light grows dimmer, the animals are not so numerous, for they cannot make their homes where the light of the sun does not reach. There are some, however, with little lanterns like the fireflies, which makes it possible for them to live in the bottom of the sea. By the aid of this dim phosphorescent light, we can just make out what is going on around u

At last, when about half a mile below the surface, we reach the floor of the sea, which stretches away in every direction like a great plain. The bottom is soft, and we sink deep into a slimy ooze which feels much like the mud in a stagnant pond.

This is a dreary place, for the waters are perfectly quiet, and the few animals move about very slowly. Our attention is attracted by little particles that are slowly sinking through the water. Most of them are so small that they look like tiny snowflakes. Has there been a storm above, and are these the little flakes of snow which disappear as they strike the water?

We hold out our hands and catch a number, and examine them closely. To our surprise we find that they are the bodies of the little animals which live in the water far above. As they grow old and die, their bodies sink down through the still water, until at last they come to rest upon the floor of the ocean.

Dipping up some of the ooze in which we stand, we see that it is formed of the same material. Living in this ooze, and feeding upon it, are worm-like animals.

Perhaps you have already thought what we ought to call this place. It is the cemetery of the sea. Here the bodies of all the animals, which are not dissolved in the water, come to rest. Among their little skeletons and shells, which are not half as big as a pinhead, there are bones of the larger animals, such as the fish and seal.

In this soft, slimy material, which is so slowly collecting, there are particles of dust from the land. A north wind whirled them into the air, and out over the ocean, and then dropped them.

Year after year the bed of ooze increases, until thousands of feet of material are deposited upon the bed of the ocean. That which is undermost, as you will readily see, must be pressed upon very heavily by that above, so that the whole mass becomes constantly harder and more compact.

Thus things went on for an unknown time in the deep ocean, which then occupied the place where the Coast Ranges now stand. Finally, these quiet times came to an end. Something strange was about to happen. There were queer sounds, and rockings of the earth, and all the animals which could, fled away.

The bottom of the sea was raised so that the bed of ooze, which during all these years had become quite hard, was raised nearly to the surface of the water. Then, from the nearest land, the ocean currents brought sand and mud, and spread them layer after layer over the surface of this old cemetery, of which we have been talking.

Long, long years passed by, and thousands of feet of sand and clay and gravels were washed on top of what was once the bed of ooze. The clays and gravels were hardened and became stone. Then another great earthquake took place, and the sea bottom was lifted high above the waters into a great range of mountains.

During the raising of the mountains, the bed of ooze was squeezed very hard, so hard that it became quite warm, and a strong smelling gas was formed from the materials of the little animal bodies. At last this gas, which is poisonous and invisible like that formed from burning coal, found some cracks in the rock through which warm water was flowing, and came to the surface. We can see it bubbling up in many of the little springs which we find in the Coast Ranges. Many birds and small animals, coming to drink at the springs, breathe the poisonous gas, and drop dead before they can get away.

There was also formed in the bed of ooze a brownish or greenish liquid. This is petroleum just as Nature gives it to us. Before it is fit to use in our lamps, it must be refined.

The crude petroleum, which is made far below the surface, soaks into the pores and cracks of the surrounding rocks, and some of it at last reaches the surface, flowing out with strong smelling springs of sulphur water. The petroleum in some of these springs is thin, and dries up like so much water, but in other springs it is very thick like tar, and gathers in large springs. The bear and deer, coming down to drink of the queer tasting water, sometimes fall into the tar, and as it is so sticky, they seldom get out.

Prospectors found hills of sandstone filled with the thick black oil, or tar, and called the sticky mass bituminous rock. The tar which they found nearly pure, and dried out so that it was hard, they called asphaltum. They discovered that it was very useful for making street pavements, and opened large quarries in different parts of the Coast Ranges, and shipped it to the cities.

Other prospectors found little streams of the thin oil flowing from the cracks in the rock, and putting up derricks, like those for windmills, they bored holes so that the oil would come out faster. The holes were made hundreds of feet deep, and sometimes they obtained one hundred barrels of oil in a day from a single well.

Over some of the springs of gas, tanks have been built for collecting it, and people have used it for lighting houses.

The oil we have used for many purposes. From one part is made naphtha and gasoline. Another part is used for burning in our lamps. From the thick portion paraffine is made, also the analine dyes, and oils for lubricating machinery.

As we look at the clear oil in our lamps, it is hard to imagine that it has had such a strange history. The little animals which lived long ago in the sea never dreamed, if they dreamed of anything, that they would be so useful.

BLACKBOARD WORDS.

Porpoise (pôr'pŭs), **ooze** (ooz), **phosphorescent** (fŏs'fŏr-ĕs'sent), **cemetery** (sĕm'ē-tĕr-y), **constantly** (kŏn'stant-lȳ), **poisonous** (poi'z'n-ŭs), **petroleum** (pĕ-trō'lĕ-ŭm), **bituminous** (bi-tū'mĕn-nŭs), **quarries** (kwŏr'riz), **naphtha** (năf'tha or năp'tha) **gasoline** (găs'ō-lin), **lubricating** (lu'bri-kāt'), **paraffine** (păr'ăf-fin).

Porpoise = a small sea animal allied to the whale.

Phosphorescent = shining without sensible heat.

Ooze = soft mud or slime.

Stagnant = not running, motionless.

Crude Petroleum = petroleum as it comes from the earth.

Tar = a soft bitumen, residue left after the evaporation of petroleum.

Naphtha, Gasoline = volatile inflammable liquids, derived from petroleum.

Lubricate = to make slippery.

Paraffine = a white, waxy substance.

Analine dye = Dyes prepared from petroleum.

IN the center of one of the desert valleys of Eastern California there is a group of men at work. The heat is almost unbearable, and they move slowly about.

What are they doing in this desolate region? They are gathering the crude borax, which forms a layer of almost dazzling whiteness over the ground as far as one can see.

We would hardly know how to get along without borax. It is useful for so many purposes. Our borax formerly came from Europe, and cost much more. Now it has been found in great abundance in the deserts of California and Nevada.

Borax goes through many processes before it is fit to use. It finally reaches us in the form of a white powder, put up in neat little packages.

The history of borax deposits, and how the crude

REFERENCE TOPICS.
Where borax is found.
How the Borax Marsh was formed.
The preparation of borax.
Marketing of borax.

material is purified and sent to market, is an interesting one.

There was a time, long ago, when more rain fell in these desert regions. The valleys had no outlets, being shut in by the mountains on all sides. As a result, the water running down the mountain cañons, flowed out into the valleys and formed lakes.

The streams carried down sand and mud, while the waves spread this material over the beds of the lakes, forming a soft, but even floor.

The streams also brought other things, such as soda and borax. These they had dissolved out of the rocks over which they flowed. The mud made the waters dirty looking, but the salt and borax were invisible, just as the salt in the ocean cannot be seen.

A time came when the lakes began to dry up. The streams were smaller, and the heat of the sun, as it poured down upon the water, evaporated more than the streams carried in.

Every year the lakes became smaller and shallower. The streams had left so much borax and soda in them during the many years since they were formed, that the water at last became unfit to drink. If you will dissolve some borax and soda in a glass you can tell how the waters of the lakes tasted.

Now set the glass out of doors, and let it stand
until the water has entirely dried out, or evaporated.
The borax and soda will appear again as a white
crust upon the bottom of the glass.

Something like this happened in these old lake-
beds. When the water had all evaporated, there
were miles and miles of mud flats. The borax and
soda which had been in the water were left mixed
with the mud.

As the mud dried upon the surface, the water
which soaked up from below kept bringing the borax
and soda, little by little, to the surface. After a time
a white layer covered the mud flats.

It looked as if there had been a snowstorm,
only the white deposit did not disappear in the hot
sun.

What a change had come over the old lake
bottom. As far as one could see, there was this
white coating over the mud flat. It glistened so
brightly in the sun as to almost blind one's eyes.

The borax deposits were not disturbed for many
centuries; but at last a prospector in crossing the
desert discovered them. Buildings were put up,
and men went to work scraping the borax into
piles.

It was then placed in large tubs of hot water
until entirely dissolved. The dirt which was mixed
with it settled to the bottom, and the water with

HAULING BORAX IN THE DESERT.

the borax was drawn off into pans, where it was allowed to cool.

In the dry air of the desert the water soon evaporated, leaving the borax in the bottom of the pans.

To get the borax to the railroad it was necessary to haul it nearly one hundred miles. Several wagons were built which would hold half as much as a freight car. They had wheels seven feet in diameter, the tires being nearly a foot wide, so that they would not sink in the sand.

Three wagons were hitched together. Two were loaded with borax, and the other carried water for the mules to drink. What a long string of mules was needed to haul these wagons. There were twenty of them. When the mules were all hitched up, and the driver had climbed into his saddle, the sight was an interesting one.

It took them three days to cross the desert, over a road which was almost as smooth and level as a railroad.

There they went, slowly creeping over the desert. All that we could see of them at first was a great cloud of dust. As they came near, the heads of the mules appeared through the dust, and then the outlines of the wagon boxes.

The mules looked dusty and tired, and so did the driver. With the creak of the wagons, and the steady sounds of the hoofs, they passed.

As the sun went down they stopped, and un-hitching the mules, made camp for the night. The precious water which the tired animals had been hauling all day was given them to drink, and they lay down to rest.

In this way the borax was taken to Mojave and placed upon the cars. When it reached Oakland it was purified farther, then ground and put in little packages for sale.

Borax not only helps in cleaning, but is useful in many other ways.

BLACKBOARD WORDS.

Borax (bō'răks), dazzling (dăz'-zlĭng), purified (pu'ri-fīd), dissolve (diz-zŏlv'), diameter (dī-ăm'ĕ-ter), Mojave (mō-hä'vä).

Borax = a compound of boracic acid and soda.

Deposit = that which is laid down or deposited from a solution.

Marsh = low, wet ground.

Soda = a white substance, having an alkaline taste.

WHERE OUR SALT COMES FROM.

AMONG the most wonderful mines in all the world, are the salt mines of Austria. There, chambers larger than houses have been dug out of the solid salt. Salt obtained in this way is called rock salt.

Salt is found in California, but here we do not have to dig underground for it.

You all know how salty the sea water is. Sailors have to carry all of their drinking water with them. If it should be used up, they would be as badly off, with the sea water all around them, as those who are lost upon the desert.

The most of our salt comes from the sea. In some places Nature has collected the salt for us upon old sea bottoms, which are now dry. In other places, we make it directly from the salt sea water.

There are many such salt works upon the eastern side of San Francisco Bay, near

REFERENCE TOPICS.
———
Source of salt.
Salt mines of Austria.
Making salt from sea water.
Salt beds in Colorado desert.

Alvarado. There the sea water is kept in ponds, and simply allowed to evaporate. You can try it yourself by placing some salt water in a basin and allowing it to stand until the water has dried up. There will then be a coating of little salt crystals over the bottom of the basin.

A marsh over which the sea water flows at high tide is selected. It is then cut into square fields by shoveling up embankments. Gates lead from one field to another, and connect with the water outside. This permits them to be filled when the tide is high.

When a pond is full of salt water the gate is closed, so that it cannot run out when the tide goes down. It is then allowed to stand for weeks in the sun, and with the winds blowing over it. When the water has nearly evaporated, the gate is again raised at high tide, so that the pond can fill up again.

This process is repeated until the salt water or brine in the pond is very strong. The water, when it passes off into the air in the form of little invisible particles, cannot carry the salt away with it. Consequently, every time the water is let in, the pond is richer in salt.

Finally, the brine is as strong as it can be made, and the salt begins to separate from the water, and fall to the bottom. You can understand more clearly now this is done by dissolving all the salt you can in a glass of water, and then allowing it to stand until some of the water has evaporated. Little crystals of salt will soon begin to appear around the sides of the glass.

When a thick layer of salt has gathered upon the bottom of the pond, the water is drawn off. Then the men go to work with shovels, and throw it out on the banks in piles.

Nature has made the great beds of salt in different parts of the world in very much the same way. We only imitate Nature when we make it by evaporating sea water.

Some of the salt beds have been buried deeply by sands and clays which have been washed over them. To get at the salt in these beds, we sometimes dig shafts, as is done in mining for coal. Men go down in these shafts, and quarry the salt. In some places, the salt water is pumped up from wells, and then allowed to evaporate as in making salt from the sea water.

When the old sea bottoms, upon which the salt lies, have not been covered up, the salt is very easy to get. This is the way the salt is found at Salton, in the Colorado Desert.

That portion of the desert which is below the level of the sea was once the head of the Gulf of Lower California, and was covered with salt water.

As the Colorado River built its delta out into the gulf, the water covering the desert became nearly cut off from the rest of the gulf.

Under the influence of the hot sun and dry air, the water was continually evaporating. To keep up the supply, the sea water flowed in from the gulf to the south. This process is, as you see, quite like that carried out artificially.

Thus the great pond or lake, for it was many miles across, at last came to form a very strong brine. After a time the delta of the Colorado River cut the lake off entirely from the Gulf of Lower California. Then the water began to dry up, and the salt to settle to the bottom, and mix with the mud.

When the clear water was all gone, the mud and salt formed a thick layer all over the bottom of the old lake. The air was so dry that the mud hardened on the surface, but it still remained soft underneath this crust.

How does the bed of pure salt form upon the surface of the former lake bottom, which is now white and glistening as far as you can see? It is in this way. You have all noticed the little salt crystals which appear upon the surface of a roll of butter when it is placed in the dry, warm air. The salt was in the butter before, but it was dissolved, and you could not see it.

The dry air brought it to the surface of the butter. There the water in which the salt was dissolved evaporated, and left the little crystals of salt.

The same thing takes place upon the bed of the old salt lake at Salton. When a layer several inches thick is formed, it is scraped up. The Indians do the most of the work in this hot region. With

SALT PLOW AT WORK AT SALTON SEA.

plows and scrapers, many hundred tons of salt are gathered every day. When the salt has been scraped into rows, it is shoveled upon the cars and taken to the mill. There it is ground and put up in form for sale.

We think it would be a very hard thing to go without salt. Yet, during some of the wars, people have been shut away from the salt beds, and have had to learn to eat their food without it.

You know how the animals like salt.   The hunter takes advantage of this fact, and waits for the deer when they come to drink at the salt licks.

BLACKBOARD WORDS.

Alvarado (ăl′vä-rä-dō), artificially (är′ti-fish′al-ly), Salton (sal′-tŏn), evaporate (ĕ-văp′ō-rāt).

Evaporate = to pass off in vapor.
Invisible = that which cannot be seen.
Imitate = to follow as a pattern, to copy.
Brine = strong salt water.
Dissolve = to become fluid; to be melted.
Salt licks = springs containing salt.

MONO LAKE.

YOU have all read of Great Salt Lake, in Utah. Its waters are so salt that if you should fall into it, it would be impossible to sink. It is a good place in which to learn to swim, although the salt is very disagreeable, if you get your head under the water.

Do you know that there is a lake in California which is fully as interesting as Great Salt Lake? It is known as Mono Lake, and lies on the edge of the desert country east of the Sierra Nevada Mountains.

Common salt is the most important substance in the water of Great Salt Lake, but our California lake contains as much soda as it does salt. You all know what soda is. It is put into biscuits to make them rise, and if there is too much of it the biscuits are yellow.

REFERENCE TOPICS.

Lakes with no outlet.
Mono Lake.
History of the lake.
Soda.
Islands in Mono Lake.
Volcanic features.

There is so much soda in Mono Lake that if the water were all evaporated, and people could get it, there would be enough to last all the bakers in the world for many years, and give everybody the dyspepsia.

There are so many queer things to be seen around Mono Lake that I will tell you about some of them.

The lake lies in an inclosed basin, without any outlet. The barren desert lies all around it, except upon the west. On that side the snowy Sierra Nevada Mountains rise very abruptly. They reach a height of a mile above the lake, while the lake itself is more than a mile above the level of the ocean.

Several dashing streams of pure, cold water from the melting snows upon the mountains flow into the lake. Nevertheless, its basin never becomes full so that streams can run out.

Where do you suppose all the water goes to? It is taken up as invisible vapor by the thirsty air, and is carried out over the hot deserts. The water of the lake is clear, and it looks as if it would be good to drink, but one little taste is enough. It is so bitter and salty.

The brooks that flow into the lake are full of trout, but if any are accidentally carried into the lake, they turn over on their backs and die immediately.

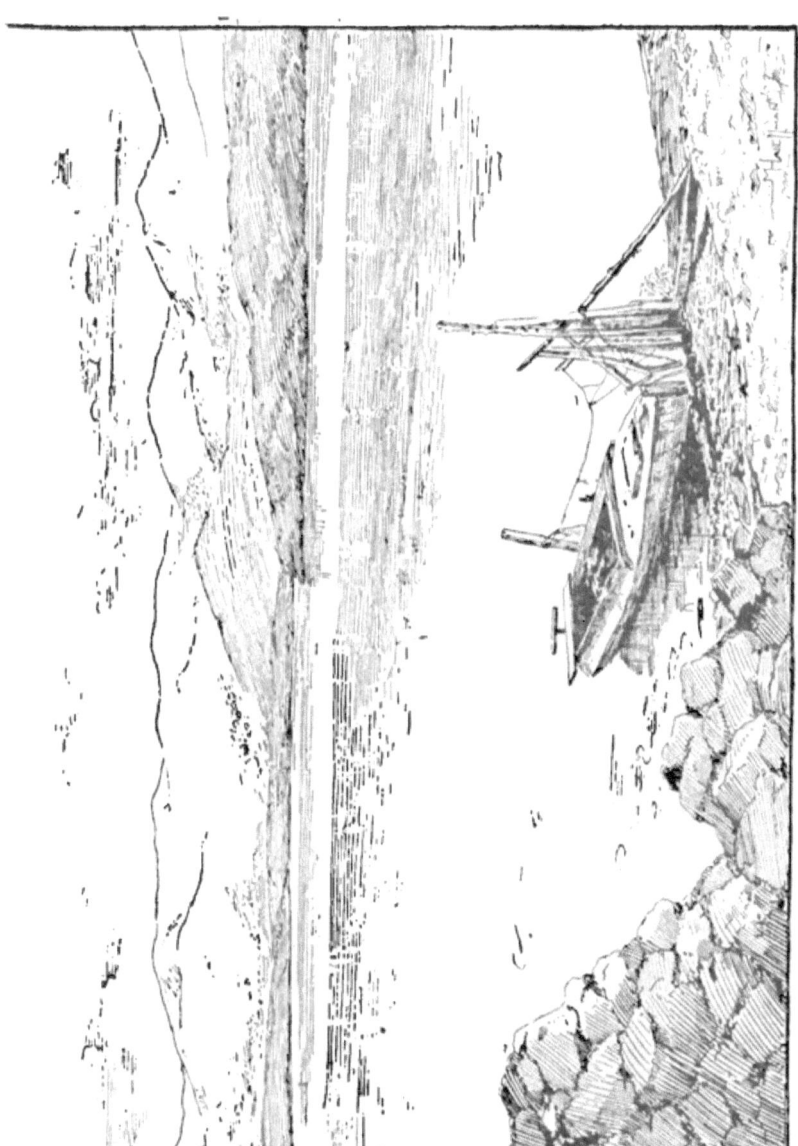

MONO LAKE—SIERRA NEVADA MOUNTAINS IN THE DISTANCE.

It is delightful water to go swimming in, for it feels so warm and soft. But you must not forget and stay in too long, for it would eat into your skin, and leave it smarting and sore.

What a washtub this great lake would make. Every afternoon when the wind blows, the waves, as they break upon the shore, raise a bank of foam looking just like soapsuds. The water is indeed very good for washing clothes, but the clothes must not be left in too long, for the water takes the color out and leaves them rotten.

Many years ago, when icy glaciers covered the Sierra Nevada Mountains, the water was higher in the lake than it is now. Pebbly beaches where the waves used to break, extend along the sides of the hills many feet above the present beach. The water then was not so full of soda and salt, and fish may have lived in it.

After the glaciers had melted, less water flowed into the lake, and it began to dry up. As the water became lower in the lake it grew more alkaline and salty. For you know that if a spoonful of salt or soda is dissolved in a pitcher of water it will not taste as strong as it would if the same amount be placed in a small dish, such as a glass.

If the water of the lake should entirely dry up, there would be left a white layer of salt and soda all over the bottom. The substances dissolved in the water do not go away with the watery vapor which the air takes up.

The water of the lake is now so strong that one would think nothing could live in it. But there is an insect which lays its eggs in this water. The larvæ, when they hatch, are thrown up by the waves along the shore, and give a very disagreeable odor. The Indians, however, think them a delicacy, and gather them in large quantities. After they are dried, they are packed away for winter use.

The region around Mono Lake is dotted with volcanoes. Although none are active now, it was different once. I am afraid we should have had as hard a time as the people of Herculaneum and Pompeii if we had lived near Mono Lake a few hundred years ago.

Streams of hot lava flowed over the country, and the volcanoes threw out clouds of pumice and ashes, which settled over everything. There must have been terrible earthquakes too.

We will visit the two islands in the lake, and see the effects of the volcanoes and earthquakes. We have to row several miles in the hot sun before reaching the first island.

There are many strange things upon these islands. Near the larger one springs of hot water come up through the lake, making a very nice place to bathe, if one does not get too near the springs. In the black lava near by, are crevices through which steam is constantly issuing with a loud, puffing noise. On a cool morning, the steam forms quite a cloud over the island.

On one of the islands is a group of craters, where explosions underneath the surface have blown the rock into fragments and left deep holes. The holes look much as they would if they had been blown out by giant powder.

In the center of the island there is a deep hole of a different kind. It certainly looks as if the bottom had fallen out.

The smaller of the islands is composed entirely of lava. It has almost no soil and only a few bushes. The island seems to have been pushed up from underneath the lake by some recent earthquake.

The rocks are shattered, and full of cracks. In the bottom of some of these there is water, and in their darker corners owls make their home.

We feel like walking lightly, for it almost seems as if the jar of our feet would send the island crumbling to the bottom of the lake.

Although the island has no springs upon it, a band of goats is kept there. They are very wild, and run like deer when we come in sight.

There are many other interesting things about Mono Lake. Many springs come up in the bottom of the lake. They carry lime dissolved in their waters, and have built up strange looking little towers. Some of these reach above the water. They are hollow inside, and the water runs up through the hollow and out over the top just like a fountain.

You may want to know where all of the salts in the lake came from. A little must have been dissolved in the spring water, but the most was brought in by the streams which flow down from the mountains. They are constantly removing a little of the rock over which they flow, and as no streams run out of the lake, everything that is brought in must stay there.

BLACKBOARD WORDS.

Glacier (glä′sher, or gläs′i-ĕr), **larvae** (lär′vē), **pitcher** (pich′er), **pumice** (pŭm-is), **Herculaneum** (her-kū-lä′ne-ŭm), **Pompeii** (pŏm pa′yē).

Substance = the material of which things are made.

Evaporate = to change a liquid into vapor.

Abruptly = suddenly.

Invisible = that which cannot be seen.

Accident = an unexpected event.

Glacier = a stream of ice slowly moving down a mountain or cañon.

Shatter = to break in pieces.

Larvae = the young, or immature stage of an insect.

Pumice = light, porous lava.

Crater = the mouth of a volcano.

THE STORY OF THE COLORADO RIVER.

SOME rivers flow through broad valleys nearly their whole length. They hardly know what a cliff or waterfall is. Others tumble and foam between steep rocks, where there is not even room for a footpath.

Different rivers can tell different stories, but there is not one that can tell a more interesting story than the Colorado. For more than two hundred miles it flows in a cañon, which is more than a mile deep, and often so narrow that the sun reaches it but a little time each day.

This great river seems almost like a living thing. It never rests, but moves on just the same, year after year. It has a great work to do, and though it has been busy for thousands of years, it has made only a small beginning.

REFERENCE TOPICS.
Locate Colorado River.
Gulf of California.
Formation of deltas.
Cañons.
Stratified rocks.
Colorado Desert.
Work of rivers.
Salton Sea.

96

THE GRAND CANON OF THE COLORADO RIVER.

The task which has been given it is enough to discourage anything but a river. It is to carry away to the sea, grain by grain, the particles which make up the mountains and plateaus which form its basin. A river basin, as you know, includes all the land sloping toward one stream.

After working all these years, it has done little more than cut this deep cañon. It has yet to carry away the material of the great plateau through which it runs.

The river does not have to work alone however, for it has many assistants. In the first place, there are the branch streams which flow into it. Each one of these grinds out a cañon for itself. As these tributary streams reach back toward the mountains which inclose the basin of the Colorado, each one in turn splits up into smaller ones. These in turn divide into little rills nourished by the springs and melting snows.

The raindrops, and the heat, and the frost are at work upon the mountains, breaking the solid rock into little fragments. These tumble into the rills, which bear them to the brooks, and the brooks give them to the rivers, which finally all unite in the yellow and muddy Colorado.

Sometimes the brooks bring more particles of sand and clay to the rivers than they can carry. Then their beds are filled up, and they overflow the valleys along their banks. But where they run swiftly, they bear along all the rubbish given to them, and keep their channels clean.

If the water of the Colorado were clear, it would have nothing with which to do its work. The sand and pebbles, which its swift current bears along, are its tools. They are rolled and shoved along the bottom, and gradually wear away the solid rock. In this way the river slowly cuts deeper into the plateau.

Each tributary stream does the same thing, so that there is formed a perfect network of cañons, which makes it impossible to travel across the country.

Here, where the great walls rise so many thousands of feet, there is a good opportunity to learn something about the rocks of which they are made. They are not massive and dark, like the lava about which we have read, but are formed of layers of different colors. The layers lie perfectly flat, like the boards in a lumber pile, and extend up and down the cañon as far as one can see.

The dark layers we will call shale. They are formed of hardened clay. The reddish layers are composed of little grains of sand, colored with something like iron rust. We will call them sandstone. Rocks made of layers in this way are said to be stratified.

Before the Colorado River existed, what is now this great plateau was beneath the sea. A river, perhaps as muddy as the Colorado, flowed into this old sea. The sand and mud, which it brought down, were washed around by the waves and currents, and spread out in layers just as we see them in the walls of the cañon.

After a time this old sea bottom was slowly and gently raised, until it was more than a mile above the surface of the water. It formed a great plateau.

Rains fell upon the plateau, and the brooks in which the drops collected ran here and there, hardly knowing, at first, what direction to take, because the surface was so level. Finally, all those upon one slope united in a valley, and flowed toward the southwest, at last reaching the Gulf of California.

In this way the Colorado River was born. It went to work at once carrying off the waste material from the hills, and at the same time cutting a cañon. It will continue this work for a long time to come.

What has the river done with all the little particles of sand and clay which it has taken from the mountains, and from the cañon? Let us follow it toward its mouth, and we may be able to learn.

When the Colorado leaves the cañon, it winds for long miles through desert hills and sandy plains. As it nears the Gulf of California, its banks become lower and more muddy. Now it enters upon a great plain, which gives place to a tidal marsh, and then to the open waters of the gulf.

This is where the river leaves its load of mud. A great delta has been formed, filling up nearly all of the northern end of the gulf. A long time ago, before the Colorado River had brought down so much mud, the Gulf of California reached north. into California. It covered what we now call the Colorado Desert.

Gradually the mud from the river spread out over the gulf until the plains of the delta extended quite across it. The very northern end of the gulf was not filled with the mud, and being cut off by the delta to the south, a salt lake was formed.

The climate in this region is very warm and dry, and little by little, the water dried up, leaving a deposit of salt. In this way the basin of the Colorado Desert was formed. The center of the basin is now about three hundred feet below the level of the sea.

When the river is high it sometimes overflows its banks, and a part of the water turns back and empties into this basin of the desert. Then a large body of shallow salt water is formed, called Salton Sea. The air is so hot and dry however, that it soon evaporates.

Little seashells are scattered at various places

over the desert. The animals which once inhabited them crawled about in the mud, when this region formed a part of the Gulf of California. Around the edges of the desert one can also trace the ancient beach, where the waves used to break.

We see now what a great work the Colorado River has done. It is still busy carrying mud and sand, and may some time fill up nearly the whole gulf.

BLACKBOARD WORDS.

Cañon (kan'yŭn), rubbish (rub bish), plateau (plȧ-tō'), lava (lä'vȧ), shale (shāl), stratified (strat'i-fīd), channel (chan'něl), delta (děl'ta) evaporate (ō-vap'ō-rāt).

Discourage = to dishearten.
Particles = small parts of anything.
Cañon : a deep gulch.
Massive = having no regular form.
Stratified = formed in layers.
Plateau = a flat, elevated area of land.
Sand = fine grains of stone.
Clay = soft, tenacious earth.
Tidal marsh = a flat covered by the ocean at high tide.

WHAT WE SAW IN AN OCEAN CLIFF.

THE picture before us represents a part of a high cliff on Point Loma, near San Diego. The shore here can be explored only at low tide, and even then it is difficult to reach.

The rocks forming the cliff are arranged in horizontal layers, and caves appear in them at different places. One of the largest of the caves is shown in the picture.

Boys always delight in exploring wild places, and Point Loma had the greatest attraction for us on this account. We discovered this cave on one of our expeditions. It was so interesting that we took a picture of it.

After exploring the cave, which extended into the rock more than one hundred feet, we sat down on the rocks. Dangling our

REFERENCE TOPICS.

Locate San Diego.
Caves.
Stratified rocks.
How stratified rocks are formed.
Earthquakes.
Fissures in the rocks.
Formation of mountains.

AN OCEAN CAVE, POINT LOMA, SOUTHERN CALIFORNIA.

feet in the water, which at ebb tide flowed back and forth very quietly, we studied the cliff and the cave.

We were interested in the regular layers of rock, formed one above the other, and wanted to know why the waves dug out a cave at this particular place.

Perhaps you would be interested, too, if we should tell you what we learned about them.

Each layer of rock is called a stratum, and the whole series is said to be stratified. Those layers which stand out sharply are harder than the others. They consist of grains of sand tightly packed together, and are called sandstone.

Those layers which have been worn away most are softer than the sandstone. They consist of clay which has been squeezed very hard. They are called shale.

These stratified rocks were formed in the bed of the ocean and then lifted up to the place in which we saw them.

You may be able to understand how they were formed if you should examine the mud flats when the tide is very low. A deep trench dug across the mud flats would show them to be made of layers like those in the cliff. They would be soft, but formed of the same materials,— sand and clay.

The little particles which make up the flat have

been brought by the waves and tides. If you turned a handful of soil into a pitcher of water the little grains of sand would go to the bottom immediately, but it would take some time for the fine particles of mud to settle.

This is the way it is in the shallow water of the flat. In the winter, when the weather is stormy and the currents strong, sand is washed onto the flat. During the long summers it is very different. The water is more quiet, and only the fine particles of mud are deposited upon the flat.

In this way, as year after year passes, you can see that a succession of layers of sand and mud would be formed in the water. The ones at the bottom would be squeezed and made hard by the weight of those above. The sand would be changed to sandstone, and the clay to shale.

Now that we have seen how the different layers in the cliff were formed, we want to know something about the cave.

The waves have dug in a long distance, and at every storm they go a little farther. At the back end of the cave is a beach of pebbles. These pebbles are the tools which the waves have been using to wear away the rock.

Study the picture carefully, and you will see a broad line upon the face of the cliff. It extends from the cave across the layers of rock, slanting upward toward the left. Along this line the rocks have been broken and ground to pieces. This is called a fault, and was formed long ago, during a heavy earthquake.

The sea bottom was being raised, when suddenly the rocks forming it broke, and those on one side of the crack slipped past those on the other. You can see from the picture that this is true, for the layers on one side do not fit those upon the other.

The waves, dashing against the cliff, found the broken place, and soon dug the clay and pieces of rock out of the crack. They kept on enlarging the hole, until the cave was formed.

Our picture teaches another very important thing. It is, that breaks of the same kind as that in the cliff have made some of the great mountain ranges of the world. Such is the origin of the Sierra Nevada, the most rugged range of mountains upon the Pacific Coast.

Perhaps you do not see how such a little crack could make a range of mountains. It is really quite simple.

Suppose you are watching a carpenter, who has stacked up a great pile of boards on two saw-horses. You can imagine that each board is a layer of rock which lies flat like those in the cliff.

Now the carpenter goes to work, and after meas-uring the boards the length he wishes, begins at the top of the pile, and saws it into two parts. There is nothing to hold up the ends of the pieces, and when the last board is cut they tip up, and one end of each part falls to the ground.

The line along which the carpenter has sawed the boards into two pieces you can imagine is a break in the crust of the earth. The end of one pile of boards slips down past the other, and forms a valley, while the parts which stick up form mountain ranges.

The Sierra Nevada Mountains are represented by the end of the pile of boards which sticks up. The great desert basin of Nevada is represented by the end of the pile which fell down.

The earthquakes which we feel may mean that the rocks have slipped past each other along a crack. While the ends of the board pile have slipped past each other only a few feet, in the Sierra Nevada Mountains the slip is in some places two miles.

Our picture of the sea cliff has made clear some of the most interesting things in the formation of the earth.

———

BLACKBOARD WORDS.

Stratum (strā'tŭm), **horizontal** (hŏr'I-zŏn'tal), **carpenter** (kär'pĕn-ter), **Sierra Nevada** (sĕ-ĕr'ra ne-vä'da).

Horizontal = parallel to the horizon; on a level.

Stratum = a bed of earth, or rock, of one kind.

Crust = the outer portion of the earth.

Shale = a sedementary rock, formed of clay, having a laminated structure.

Sandstone = a rock made of grains of sand cemented together.

Ebb tide = the flowing back of the tide.

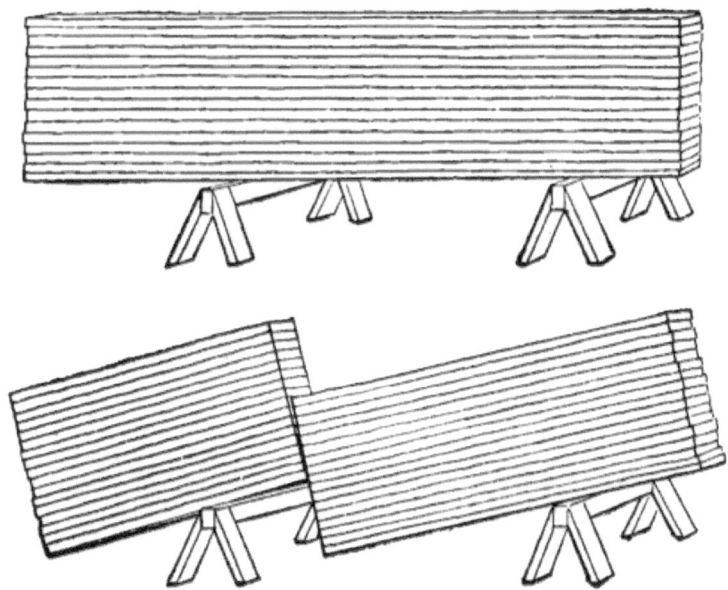

HOW ISLANDS ARE FORMED.

ISLANDS are interesting things. What fun it is to discover an island, and play Robinson Crusoe. The island may be nothing more than a sand bar, or a little bare rock, but for the boys it is an island just the same. It calls up pictures of shipwrecks in some far away part of the world.

Islands are made in different ways, but if there were no water there could be no islands at all.

Suppose we try to imagine our globe without any water. Its whole surface would be made up of mountains, valleys, and plains. Now, if on this dry world it should rain torrents for years and years, the water would run into all the lowest places, and form the oceans which are spread out before us.

If more water were

REFERENCE TOPICS.

What are islands.
Water necessary.
Ways in which islands are made.
Work of the waves.
The tools of the waves.

110

ROCKY ISLANDS, NEAR POINT BUCHON, ON THE COAST OF CALIFORNIA.

turned into the oceans, they would rise higher, and cover up more of the land. There are mountains beneath the sea just as on the land, only they are not high enough to rise above the water.

The continents are the large bodies of land which stick up out of the water. The small ones are called islands. You can easily see that if there were more water, many of the islands would be entirely covered and hidden from sight. If there were less water, new islands would stick their heads up.

You have seen the same thing happen in the rivers in the summer time. As the water goes down, many little islands and sand bars come into sight, and some of these you can finally walk out to without wetting your feet.

There is another very different way in which islands are formed.

If you have ever visited the sea shore, you have seen how the waves are always beating against the rocks. Sometimes the waves are small, and break very gently, but in stormy weather it is different.

Water by itself cannot wear away the hard rocks. It is only when the waves have something to work with that they accomplish anything.

The tools of the waves are grains of sand, pebbles, and bowlders, which lie along the shore. As each wave runs back you can hear the rumble of the pebbles rolling down the beach. When the next wave comes, it picks them up and hurls them with great force against the cliffs.

With each blow a little of the rock is ground from the cliff. When the waves have succeeded in wearing out a hollow at the bottom, the cliff caves down. Each new fragment of the rock cliff falling into the ocean is in turn used as a hammer by the waves. In this way they slowly eat into the land. They grind it away little by little, in the form of sand and mud, which the currents of water then spread over the ocean bottom.

On some sea coasts the land is being destroyed so fast that houses, and even whole farms, are washed away.

But you may ask what has this to do with the making of islands. Look closely at this picture of a wild part of the California coast, and perhaps you can tell. The first thing which will attract your attention are some rocky islands, with the waves foaming all about them. At the right side of the picture is the mainland with which the islands were once connected. The broad strip of water in the front of the picture was formerly occupied by the land.

The waves hunt out all the soft places in the rocky cliffs, just as you would do if the same work were given you. They hurl the bowlders and pebbles against the cliffs, and dig caves and passage-ways where the soft spots are.

After a long time the shore is dug into so far that bays are formed, where little boats may anchor safely. But the harder rocks remain as headlands, or capes, between the bays.

The waves continue to beat against the rocks, until some of the headlands are left entirely surrounded by water. This is the way the islands which appear in the picture were made. How boldly and defiantly they face the storms. At first, they are only a little distance from the mainland, but as the waves keep at work they are left farther and farther out in the ocean.

The waves have a long task ahead of them to tear the islands down. The water is quite deep about them, and the pebbles have been washed toward the shore.

Under the attack of the atmosphere and waves the islands will finally crumble away, and in the place of each there will be left only a reef upon which the waves will break in stormy weather.

New islands will be formed as long as the waves continue to tear down the cliffs.

Islands assume strange shapes sometimes. If you will examine the picture carefully, you will see that the island farthest away looks very much like a lion at rest. It is called Lion Rock.

What picturesque rocky hills these islands would make if the sea should retreat and leave them upon the dry land. I suppose that all children who know anything about the sea, and have wandered along the shore, have wished that they could explore the bottom, and climb up on the rocky reefs and islands.

The sea birds use the islands for nesting places, and cover them with the white guano which is so valuable for making land produce heavier crops.

The sea lions and seals also make use of the islands, for they are more protected from hunters. At certain seasons of the year nearly all the rocky islands along the coast of California are inhabited by the bellowing sea lions.

BLACKBOARD WORDS.

Anchor (an'kĕr), **picturesque** (pik'tŭr-ĕsk'), **guano** (gwa'nō).

Hurl = to throw.

Pebbles = small, rounded stones.

Bowlders = like pebbles, but much larger.

Beach = a sandy, or pebbly, shore.

Defiantly = boldly, insolently.

Crumble = to break into small pieces.

Guano = deposits left by birds upon shores or islands.

Sea lion = a species of seal.

Seal = an aquatic mammal.

THE STORY OF THE YOSEMITE VALLEY.

HE fame of the Yosemite Valley has gone all over the world. People travel thousands of miles for the purpose of spending a few days there, looking at the cliffs and waterfalls.

What is there about this valley which makes it so attractive? There are cliffs and waterfalls in other places.

We can tell best, if we see the valley with our own eyes. It is a long ride, up and down wooded mountains, and by roaring streams, into the very heart of the Sierra Nevada Mountains.

We begin to wonder where the valley is, when all at once, passing a turn in the road, we come out on the edge of a great precipice.

Far below, so far that the pine trees look like little bushes, lies the beautiful Yosemite Valley. There are green meadows and forests, through which winds a shining river.

REFERENCE TOPICS.

Discovery of the Yosemite.
Character of the valley.
How formed.
Work of the streams.
Work of the glaciers.

116

On every side of the valley rise walls of rock. In some places, they are almost a mile high. At several points little streams, flowing down from the higher mountains about the valley, tumble in streaks of foam over the walls of rock.

The valley seems like a picture in a frame of bare granite mountains, and you wonder how it came there.

Some people have thought that, during an earthquake a long time ago, the bottom fell out of the mountains, and left the deep hole in which the valley now lies. We do not think this is the way it was formed. We think the brooks and rivers can tell us more about how it was done.

A long time ago the Sierra Nevada Mountains were not so high as they are now. There were no deep cañons, and bare granite peaks, but in their places valleys and rolling hills.

Then something began to lift the hills higher and higher. They became colder, and it snowed and rained a great deal. This gave the rivers much to do. They could no longer play truant in shady ponds, as they used to do. They had to run more swiftly to reach the San Joaquin Valley, and dashed from rock to rock over their rough beds.

The streams said to themselves, if we can only wear the rocks away, and dig deep gorges between the mountains, we shall then not have to run so fast, and besides, we shall be hidden from the sun the most of the day.

They went to work with a will, and by the aid of the sand and pebbles, which the brooks brought them, they ground away the rocks over which they flowed, and in this way cut deep channels.

Those rivers, which were the largest, and flowed over the softest rock, accomplished the most, and at last hid themselves deep down between the mountain walls.

In this way the Merced got ahead of its brother rivers, and dug out the beautiful Yosemite Valley. It had to carry away much material, for the valley is eight miles long, and more than a half a mile wide and deep. But it did it, nevertheless, by taking the rock away, a few grains at a time. The most of this waste was left in the San Joaquin Valley, and it is this which makes the great valley smooth as a floor.

The Merced River had many tributaries, as it flowed through the Yosemite Valley, but they were small, and did not cut down into the granite rock as fast as the main river did. So, in order to get to the river, they had to jump over the great walls about the valley. In this way, the pretty water-falls were formed. Some of them are so high that the water turns to spray before it reaches the bottom of the valley.

Now that the valley was cut out, the Merced River felt quite happy. Its work was almost done. But disappointment came to the river as it does to people. The climate continued to grow colder, and it snowed so much, that it seemed to the river that the whole world must be covered by the white sheet.

In the winter, the water of the river froze, and it could not run, but in the summer it had to do double work, because of the melting snows.

After a time more snow fell in the winter than could melt the coming summer, and it increased so much that it began to slide down the mountain sides and to fill up the cañons which the rivers had dug.

The snow became hard and icy like the snow-balls which the boys have made on a warm afternoon and left out over night to freeze. The valley of the Merced River was filled at last with the ice. It moved along so slowly that one would have had to watch it a long time to be sure that it did move.

You can imagine how the ice acted by watching a little stream of molasses on a cold morning, only that the molasses is sticky, while the ice was not.

Such a stream of ice is called a glacier, and this cold time upon the mountains the Glacial period.

How the glacier did tear the mountain sides as it moved down the valley! It broke off all the projecting points of rock and scraped them along, polishing the old bed of the river and the sides of the cañon.

For many years the ice filled the valleys, and they would surely have been forgotten if any one had lived in California then.

The cold came to an end, however, and the ice melted away, giving the valley over to the river again.

The river hardly recognized its old home. Everything was greatly changed. All the trees and soil had been carried away by the ice, and there was nothing but barren granite. How the granite did shine in the sunlight! It was polished in many places as smooth as a mirror.

The river did not have as quiet a time in the Yosemite Valley as it used to. Great bowlders, which the glacier had dropped, were strewn all over it, and the river had to hunt for a new channel.

The river went to work to make the valley smooth and fertile as it was before, but it was very slow work. The ice had swept every bit of soil from the mountain slopes, and it was some time before the rain and frost could pry the particles of the rock apart, and furnish sand and clay for the brooks to carry to the river.

At last the river succeeded in covering up the

most of the bowlders in the valley, and grass and trees sprang up. Innumerable bright flowers covered the bottom lands, and in the meadows the red strawberries grew without any one but the birds to eat them.

What a happy valley this was, all shut in from the outside world! The wild animals made it their home, but there was no one to see the grand cliffs and beautiful waterfalls. The animals thought only of something to eat and a comfortable home in the winter. The brooks, as they jumped over the cliffs in haste to join the river in the valley below, sang to the empty air.

Time went on, until some Indians, hunting through the woods which had grown up on the surrounding mountains, accidentally came to the edge of the cliffs and looked over.

The valley seemed so inviting that they went back for their friends; then they all climbed down the steep walls into the valley, and made their homes there.

When the miners came to the mountains, the Indians frequently went out on stealing expeditions. They were often followed, but for a long time succeeded in escaping to their well-hidden homes.

One day they were less fortunate, and were traced to the valley, where a fight took place. The miners

drove the Indians out and took possession of the
beautiful valley.

It was so difficult to get into the valley, that for a
long time but little was known about it.   When the
rude trails were replaced by smooth roads, many
people went to visit it, and the story of the wonderful valley spread all over the world.

BLACKBOARD WORDS.

Yosemite (yŏ-sĕm'ĭ-tē), **gorge** (gôrj), **accomplished** (ăk-
kŏm'plĭsht) **San Joaquin** (săn-wah-keen), **tributary** (trĭb'ū-
tā-ry), **glacier** (glā'sher or glăs'ĭ-er), **recognized** (rĕk'ŏg-nīz'd),
polished (pŏl'-ĭsht), **strewn** (strun or strŏn), **expedition** (ĕks
pē-dĭsh'ŭn), **possession** (pŏz-zĕsh'ŭn), **fortunate** (fôr'tū-nāt).

Tributary = a stream flowing into a larger river or lake.
Granite = a rock formed of quartz, feldspar, and mica.
Gorge = a narrow passage between mountains.
Fertile = fruitful, productive.
Trail = a path or road through a wild region.

WHEN THE MASTODON LIVED.

MOST of us have seen the elephant, with his curious trunk, great dangling ears, and stumpy legs. How alarmed we should be to meet some day a number of these animals roaming wild in the woods!

If we had lived here several thousand years ago, however, we should have become as used to elephants as the people of Africa and India now are.

We cannot realize how long a time a thousand years is, for even one year seems to pass so slowly. All that we can know is that a long time ago, when our Pacific Coast home was very different, many strange animals lived here. Among them was one great animal in particular, which looked much like the ele-

REFERENCE TOPICS.

Fossil bones.
The mastodon.
Animals living with the mastodon.
The glacial period.
Santa Barbara Islands.
The teeth of plant-eaters. (See text-books upon geology.)

123

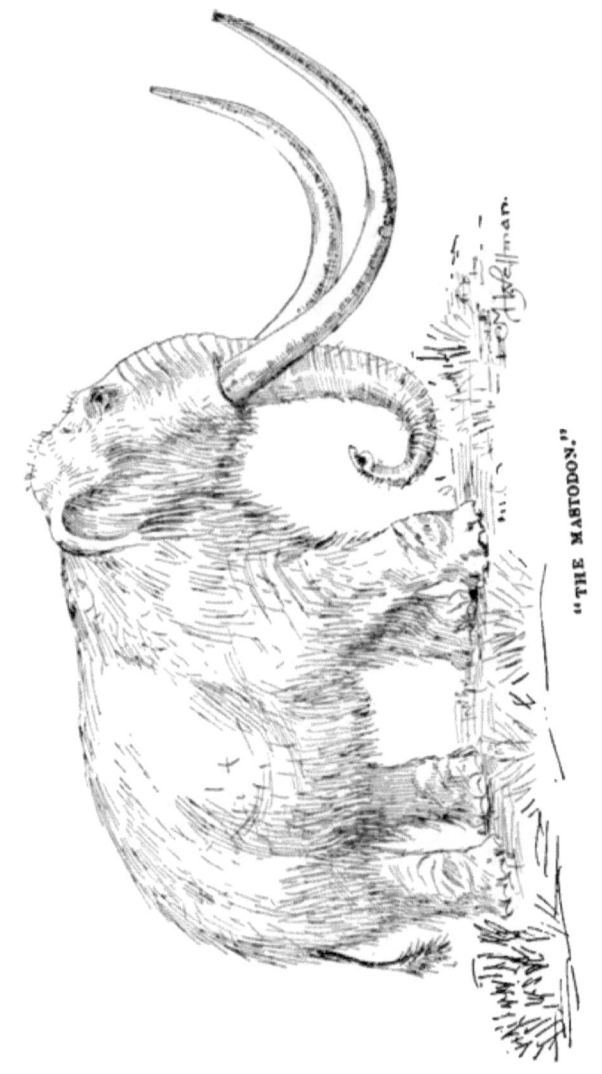

"THE MASTODON."

phant, only that it was larger, had long shaggy hair and great curved tusks.

We have read of such animals having been found frozen in the snow of the far north, but what reason have we to suppose that they ever lived in California?

It came about in this way. One of the streams where we used to fish had been swollen by days of heavy rain, and as it rushed along, it tore away the grassy bank in many places. Half a mile below the house it formed a cliff, about forty feet high. Here we went to hunt for the smooth and prettily colored pebbles which had washed out of the bank.

One day we found that the water had exposed something very different. There were some giant bones sticking out of the hard clay, some fragments of tusks, teeth as large as our heads, and leg bones fully four feet long.

We had never seen an animal which was as large as this one must have been when it was alive. Even the elephant at the show could not have stood more than half as high. We had heard stories of great animals which had lived here before people came, but they never seemed true. It was said that these animals roamed about our home in the foothills, eating the leaves and branches of the trees, and that when they died their bones were covered up in the gravel of the creeks or in the mud of the lakes.

We asked an old man, who seemed to know a great deal, to come and help us dig the bones out. When they were all lying on the bank we sat down to rest, and he told us many things about this animal and the time when it lived.

He said that these fossil bones belonged to a mastodon, and that it lived so long ago that we would grow tired trying to think how long. He said also that we would not have known the country around our home. The most of the plants and trees were different, and there were many other strange animals besides the mastodon.

This was all so new to us, and so interesting, that we wanted to know more about those times, and so he continued.

Before the mastodon lived here the country was warm, and the mountains not so high as they are now. But there came a time when the land began to rise, and as it rose the climate became colder, until snow, instead of rain, fell on all the hills and mountains.

Jack Frost, who loves cold weather, gradually extended his kingdom over all the high mountains of the Pacific Coast. Every winter it became a little colder and a little more stormy. The winter snows grew deep, and covered up all the bare rocks, and at last, even the tallest trees were completely hidden. The animals and birds who made their homes in the mountains, either died or moved into the valley, where it was still warm.

The country kept rising, until the shore of the ocean was farther west. It was at last all dry land between the Santa Barbara islands and the present mainland.

What a strange looking country it was. The mountains, so cold and white, rose above the valleys where trees and grasses abounded, and all sorts of queer animals chased each other through the brush or nibbled the grass of the meadows.

There were several kinds of elephant-like animals, of which the mastodon was the largest. The teeth that we have found show us that these animals were plant-eaters, for the surfaces of the teeth are flat, and fit for grinding the leaves and stems of plants rather than for tearing flesh.

We can picture to ourselves herds of these clumsy, shaggy creatures as they fed upon the brush in some shady spot. All at once, perhaps, they start to run, as a lion, as fierce as any in the African jungle, bounds into their midst, and the earth shakes beneath their great feet.

In another place might be seen a group of animals, appearing much like the camel, only larger. They were the ancestors of the llama, of South America, which the Indians use for pack-animals.

In addition to the sloth and tapir, which are not

found now in North America, there were wild hogs and wolves and deer. The ferocious looking buffalo may also be added to our picture.

Two kinds of wild horses wandered through the larger valleys. One of them was a third larger than any living now. We wonder what has become of them, for when America was discovered there were no wild horses here. The great bands of horses which used to roam over the plains of Texas and South America descended from the horses which the Spaniards brought over with them.

The ice and snow covered the mountains for many centuries. At last a change came. Not so much snow fell during the winter, and in the summer more of it melted, so that the rocky peaks began to appear here and there. The glaciers, which are only streams of ice, melted slowly, and the rivers were high and thick with mud.

The climate changed in the valleys. The animals of which we have been talking did not seem so numerous. Many of them were sensitive to changes, and as less rain fell, and the plants began to dry up, they disappeared one by one. Some of these animals went to other regions and some died. Many skeletons were scattered around in the sun; these soon decayed and disappeared. A few were preserved by being buried in the swamps and river bottoms. These are the ones which we often find to-day.

The mastodons and other animals, as they fed here and there, had wandered out to the region of the Santa Barbara islands. When the climate became warmer, it was because of the fact that the land was sinking. So, by and by, the sea again flowed in through the Santa Barbara channel and cut the animals off, so that they could not retreat to the mainland. They died there, and the rains washed soil over many of their skeletons. The waves are now at work tearing down the islands, and as they wash away the cliffs, the buried bones of these old animals are frequently exposed.

As the climate continued to grow warm, different plants and animals took the places of those that had died, for we know that every living thing is adapted to the place in which it is found.

The plants which had come down from the north with the cold of the Glacial period, for that is what we call the time when the mountains were so snowy, retreated as the snow melted. We still find a few of them living on the highest mountains, where the cold yet remains.

For many long years after the ice and snow left the mountains, they showed nothing but bare rock. Little by little the soil gathered, the winds and birds carried seeds, and the trees, bushes, and grasses began to grow. With the new vegetation came the animals which are now living here.

Since the Pacific Coast has been settled, we have found large numbers of the bones of the animals which used to live here. Having the bones, we can tell a great deal about those ancient times. Do you not think it is interesting to know what happened on our earth long before we were here?

Summer and winter succeeded each other many times, and California came to look much as it does now. We are not certain that the Indians lived here with the mastodon, but they must have had their homes here for centuries before the early explorers came.

After what our wise old friend had told us, the great bones upon the bank seemed full of stories of the past. We imagined them alive again, and clothed with flesh, and the mastodon feeding in the valley, at the foot of the snowy mountains.

BLACKBOARD WORDS.

Elephant (ĕl'ō-fant), mastodon (măs'tō-dŏn), fossil (fŏs'-sil), jungle (jŭn'g'l), llama (lä'ma), sloth (slōth), tapir (tā'per) centuries (sĕn'tū-riz), glacier (glā'sher).

Mastodon = an extinct animal, related to the elephant.
Fossil = the remains of an animal dug from the earth.
Jungle   a dense growth of brushwood, grasses, etc.

Glacier = a stream of ice, slowly moving down a mountain or valley.

Llama = an American ruminant, allied to the camel, but with no hump.

Tapir = a hoofed animal, with five toes on the front feet and three on the hind feet.

Climate = the condition of a place with reference to heat and moisture.

Glacial Period = a time when large glaciers covered the northern and central portions of America and Europe.

THE MAKING OF MOUNTAINS.

E have learned from our study of the ocean cliff, that earthquakes and the formation of long cracks in the earth, have much to do with the making of some kinds of mountains. We have also learned how great volcanoes like Mount Shasta are built up.

There is still another way in which mountains arise, and we can understand it by studying an apple.

We have all noticed how wrinkled the skin of an apple becomes when it stands for a time in the dry air. The apple shrinks, because some of the juice evaporates. The skin is then left too large, and as it clings tightly to the pulp underneath, it is finally obliged to wrinkle.

Nearly all the substances of which the earth is made,

REFERENCE TOPICS.
A shrinking apple.
Original condition of the earth.
A cooling earth.
Effect upon the crust.
Folded strata.
The formation of mountains.

shrink as they become cooler, and expand with increase of heat. The earth, as you have learned, was once hot all over. It has now become cold, and hard upon the outside, but it is still hot and soft inside. This inner part of the earth far below us is cooling all of the time, and as it does so, it shrinks, leaving the hard crust upon which we stand, too large.

Now, what happens? The crust has to settle down, and in doing so, it forms folds, just as the skin does upon an apple.

A large part of the crust of the earth is arranged in layers. There are layers of pebbles, sandstone, clay, and other rocks. These, when they are formed in the bed of an ocean or lake, are nearly level. When the crust of the earth folds, these layers are tipped up at all sorts of angles.

We cannot go into the cañons in any portion of the Coast Ranges without seeing these layers standing more or less steeply. It is easy to make some of the wrinkles or folds, in the same way that those upon the earth are made. We will take some sheets of paper, and holding the opposite sides in each hand, shove them together. The paper will bend in folds.

The folds upon the earth are sometimes so large that they form high mountains. We can often see the layers arching like a rainbow upon the sides of the cañons.

Our picture shows some folded rocks upon the coast of California. These layers of sandstone, which are now folded into the form of a letter S, were once flat and even. We can hardly imagine what a great force it requires to bend solid rocks in this manner.

If the skin of an apple consisted of layers, they would appear folded, just as the rocks are in the picture.

A SHRUNKEN APPLE.

AN EXTINCT VOLCANO.

WE have all been startled at some time or other by the sudden escape of steam from the safety-valve of an engine.

With a loud, explosive noise, the steam bursts out for a moment, and then stops.

The engine-boiler is made in such a way that, when the pressure of the steam inside has reached the limit of safety, some of it can escape. If it were not for the safety-valve, the boiler might be blown to pieces.

Did you ever think that there are mountains on our earth which behave much like the safety-valve of an engine? Such mountains are called volcanoes.

The ground over which we walk seems perfectly firm and solid, yet the

REFERENCE TOPICS.
———
The cause of volcanoes.
How volcanoes are made.
A volcano in action.
Extinct volcanoes.
Mount Shasta.
Cascade Range.
Late volcanic eruption in California. (See Physiography of the United States for further information.)

earthquakes which shake it once in a while, and the volcanic eruptions, teach us that there are giant forces shut up within it.

Miles below our feet the heat is so great that the rocks are melted, just as the iron is in a furnace. There is steam in those regions also, and it is trying to get out in the same way that the steam tries to get out of the engine-boiler.

Water soaks down through the rocks to these hot regions, and is there changed to steam. When the pressure of the steam becomes too great, it blows a hole through the crust of the earth at some weak spot.

The steam is mixed with the melted rock or lava, and when it makes a hole to the surface, the whole mass is blown high in the air. This is the beginning of a volcano.

Some of the lava is blown into pieces so small that they seem like dust, and float many miles before settling to the ground. These fine particles are called volcanic ashes.

The heavier pieces do not float away in the wind, but fall back around the mouth of the volcano. Some of them look like masses of slag from a furnace, and are known as cinders. Others are heavy and round like cannon balls, and are called bombs.

This material gradually builds up a rim about the opening. The basin-like depression thus formed in the center is called the crater.

Mount Shasta is the most perfect of the great volcanoes upon the Pacific Coast. There it stands in Northern California, so tall and grand, a giant among the other mountains. Through the long summer, its cap of pure white snow attracts you. Is there anything so wonderful as this great mountain rising three miles above the level of the sea?

Yet a long time ago this mountain began as a little volcano. If we could have stood then upon the top of the mountain, and looked down into the crater, we would have seen some interesting things taking place.

We would have seen the red-hot lava with the steam rising from its surface, once in a while settling down almost out of sight in the throat of the volcano, and showing a tube-like opening leading down into the earth.

Then the lava would rise again, bubbling with the escaping steam, just as a pudding does. As each bubble broke, a great cloud of steam would escape.

When more steam had formed than could escape in this way, it would gradually lift the whole mass of lava, until boiling and foaming, it would run over the lowest place in the rim of the crater, and down the side of the mountain.

If we had been there when the explosions took place, it would have been very dangerous. We should have had to crawl under some projecting rock, to escape being hit by the chunks of the falling lava, which had been blown into the air.

The heat, the steam, the poisonous air, and the glare of the lava at night, would have been terrifying. Then, when the explosions took place, it would have seemed as if the whole mountain were being blown into the air.

Just watch your mother make a hasty pudding some day, and you will get an idea of how the lava acts. If the bubbles of steam should blow some of the hot pudding in your face, it will seem all the more real.

A volcano not only acts like a safety-valve, but like a cannon as well. The steam blows the lava up through the throat of the volcano, as powder does the shot from the cannon. The comparison is all the more real, because the masses of lava hurled into the air are called bombs.

Some of the lava which flowed out cooled around the top. This, together with the chunks which were thrown out, slowly built up the top of the volcano. At last, it towered high above all the surrounding mountains.

How the ashes and lava desolated the country around the volcano! One stream of lava reached the cañon of the Sacramento River, and followed it for nearly fifty miles. The heat of the lava turned the river to steam, and not until the lava cooled could the river flow there again.

The lava was so hard, that when the river did begin to flow again, it cut a new channel by the side of the old one, which the lava had filled up.

Mount Shasta now stands there so quiet, it is hard to imagine the exciting events of its history. All the volcanoes along the line of the Cascade Range, including Mt. Hood and Mt. Rainier, are now extinct. By that we mean that the lava in their throats has become cold and hard, and the openings far down into the earth, through which the steam hurled the lava, are closed.

Mount Shasta was the last of these volcanoes to become extinct. It has probably not been so, very many centuries, for there are several places upon its summit where the hot sulphurous gases still issue from the crevices in the lava. In fact, we are not quite sure that Mount Shasta is extinct. It may break out again some time.

You know that Vesuvius, that great volcano on the Bay of Naples, was supposed to be extinct nearly two thousand years ago. The people, who lived there, had no traditions of its ever having been in eruption. They built villages and set out vineyards on its slopes.

It broke forth again, without warning, in the year 79 A.D. Streams of lava flowed down the mountain, destroying everything in their path. Clouds of volcanic ashes also fell, burying whole cities, which remained there undisturbed for centuries until they were almost forgotten.

Near Lassen's Peak, which is also a volcano, there is a stream of lava which must have issued from the earth not more than two hundred years ago. The trunks of pine trees, which were killed by the falling ashes, are still standing.

If Mount Shasta is really a dead volcano, the rain, and frost, and little rivulets, will gradually tear it down. They are at work upon it now, but so slowly do they work, that it will be many centuries before they will succeed in affecting it very much.

BLACKBOARD WORDS.

Valve (vălv), **volcano** (vŏl-kā′nō), **cinder** (sin′der), **bombs** (bŏms or bŭms), **terrifying** (tĕr′ri-fī′-ing), **explosion** (ĕks-plo′zhŭn), **centuries** (sĕn′tū-riz), **extinct** (ĕks-tinkt′).

Valve = a lid opening only one way.

Steam = the vapor of boiling water.

Foam = an aggregation of bubbles upon the surface of a liquid.

Extinct = extinguished, put out.

CAVES.

HAT delights the boys most when they are climbing among the rocks is to find a cave. There is something very attractive to them about a hole in the ground. They want to explore it at once, and see where it leads to.

It may be that boys like caves so well because our ancestors used to live in them, and found them of great protection at many times.

In rocky countries, many animals make their permanent homes in caves. The greatest caves that we know anything about are in Kentucky. The largest is the Mammoth Cave, in which one can walk for miles without ever coming out to the light. Caves like these in the limestone are made by running water. The rain water soaks down through the soil and into the cracks in the limestone. Little by little it

REFERENCE TOPICS.

Mammoth Cave.
Kinds of caves.
Caves in the lava.
Effect of caves upon surface water.
Streams in caves.

143

MOSS BRAE FALLS.

dissolves the rock, and after a time great caverns are formed, through which the streams run.

There are a few caves in the limestone upon the Pacific Coast, but no very large or interesting ones.

Many caves are formed in other ways. Ocean waves are interested in caves. They have slowly worn them out of the cliffs, against which they are perpetually dashing.

Ocean caves were years ago, the favorite resort of smugglers and pirates, and many interesting stories have been written about them.

Some of the caves into which the ocean used to dash are now above the reach of the waves. That many of them have been used as camping-places by the Indians, is shown by the smoked walls.

The most interesting caves are found in the lava-fields of the Northwest. The lava rocks which cover so much of Northeastern California, Oregon, and Washington are full of holes and cracks and underground passage-ways.

There are many things which make us believe that there are caves all over this region. In riding over the lava, the rock frequently sounds hollow under the horses' feet. Besides this, there is little surface water for miles. The water from the snow and rain, runs into the cracks in the lava and gathers in underground streams.

In some places the caves have fallen in, and we can actually explore them.

These caves are very different from those in the limestone on the seashore. They were not made by water, but by the lava when it cooled, and the water has simply made use of them.

Some of the underground passages must be many miles in length. North of Mount Shasta there is one called Pluto's Cave. It was formed by a long, narrow stream of lava. A crust of solid lava formed on the outside of the stream while it was still hot and soft inside. What do you suppose happened then? It was a very strange thing. The inside flowed on and left the hardened shell. Thus a long hollow tube was formed, which looked on the inside something like a railroad tunnel.

This cave has been followed more than a mile without finding the end. It is very rough inside, and the walls, where they have not caved, show the hollows and ridges of the crust. The cave is in places eighty feet high and seventy feet broad.

It is a queer sensation to climb through one of these caves, where a red-hot and steaming lava stream once flowed.

In the Modoc lava-beds there are many such caves partly broken in. It is here, you will remember, that Captain Jack and the Modoc Indians took their stand against the soldiers. The Indians took refuge in the caves, where there was plenty of water. They knew the country perfectly, and it would have taken an army to have driven them out.

The caves through which the underground streams flow are generally too small to explore, besides, one would be troubled with the water. Many of them are deep under the lava, and would never be known if it were not for the cañons which cross this region.

The cañons have been formed by the larger rivers flowing across the lava-beds. Many of the streams underneath the lava are thus exposed. Some of them are so large that we might call them rivers. A perfect torrent of water pours out of an underground passage in the cañon of the upper McCloud River. The volume of water is so great that it doubles the size of the stream.

Moss Brae Falls, in the cañon of the Sacramento River, has the same origin. It comes, under the lava, from Mount Shasta, fully twenty miles away. The water is pure, and almost ice-cold. It never sees the light of day after leaving the melting snows high on the slope of Shasta until it runs down over the fern-covered ledges into the Sacramento River.

Other large springs issue from under the ends of lava-beds. Springs of this kind form Fall River, an important tributary of the Pitt River. An interesting feature of rivers that are formed of such springs is that they flow nearly the same size the year around.

One of the springs which forms Fall River is so large that it has been used to run a saw-mill.

Other springs of equal size are scattered all along the base of the Cascade Range.

All these things show us that caves are among the most interesting features of the lava-beds.

BLACKBOARD WORDS.

Attractive (ăt-trăkt'-ĭv), **favorite** (fā'ver-ĭt). **soldier** (sōl' jer), **tributary** (trĭb'ū-tā-ry), **feature** (fē'tūr).

Limestone = a rock made of carbonate of lime.

Mt. Shasta = an extinct volcano, in Northern California.

Modoc Lava Beds = A rugged field of lava in Northeastern California.

Smuggler = one who brings into, or ships goods out of a country without paying duties.

Pirate = one who robs on the seas.

Explore = to search carefully.

CRATER LAKE.

UR world is very old, and many things have happened upon it since it began moving around the sun. We would have opened our eyes very wide at some of these things if we had been there to see them.

The ocean now covers sunken continents, where wild animals once roamed and trees waved their branches in the wind. Sea shells upon the mountain tops tell an equally wonderful story of sea bottoms which have become dry land.

There was a time, long before people lived upon the earth, when central Oregon was beneath the sea. The ocean did not always remain there, however, for earthquakes occurred and great cracks opened in its bed. From these cracks flowed streams of melted lava, which slowly cooled, and as the years

REFERENCE TOPICS.
Locate Cascade Mountains.
Volcanoes.
Mount Mazama.
Crater.
History of Crater Lake.
Features of the lake.

149

CRATER LAKE, SOUTHERN OREGON.

went on were heaped one upon the other, until the Cascade Mountains were formed.

On the summit of these mountains, and rising many thousand feet higher, were the great volcanoes which we call Shasta, Mazama, Rainier, and Hood, besides many smaller ones.

All but Mt. Mazama you will find marked upon the maps. This was a great mountain, almost as high as Shasta; and you ask why it is not down also. Simply because no such mountain exists there to-day. In its place is Crater Lake. Listen, and I will tell you the strange story of Mt. Mazama.

For centuries Mt. Mazama poured out smoke, ashes, and streams of lava. At last, the fire nearly died out in the mountain, and only now and then a little steam issued from its top. The rough and jagged lava rocks upon its slopes grew cold.

The climate became cold, and the Cascade Mountains were covered with snow and ice all the year round. What is now the Willamette Valley was then a lake. Long streams of ice, formed from the hardened and partly melted snow, moved slowly down the mountains to the lake, and breaking off, floated out upon its surface.

The region all about Mt. Mazama was a desolate one. All the vegetation, even the tallest trees, were buried under the snow. No living thing was to be seen, except when some Arctic animal wandered over it.

After a time the climate grew warmer, and the snow melted away. Grass and bushes, and finally trees, covered the mountains again.

A family of bears, searching for a home, came to a deep cave under the lava on the slope of Mt. Mazama, and stopped there. The home was well chosen, for during the cold winters the bears retreated far into the cave, where the snow could not reach them.

During the summers they had the huckleberries, which grew in the meadows, a little farther down the mountain, all to themselves, for the most of the other animals, as well as the birds, seemed afraid of the mountain.

The years passed happily, until the bears began to be suspicious that something was going on within the mountain. Strange rumblings were heard, and the rocks often trembled. Once the mouth of the cave was nearly closed by a rock which had rolled down. In the winters the heat began to disturb their long sleep, so that more than once they thought spring had come, when it was still midwinter.

Finally, one night, when returning from an expedition, they saw the sky above the summit of the great mountain on which they lived, lighted up brightly, and shortly after, fine, suffocating ashes began to fall.

At last, when an unusually heavy earthquake shook the cave, our family of bears could stand it no longer, and started pell-mell down the mountain side to find a safer place.

In the days that followed the heat increased. There were loud, thundering noises, and earthquakes so severe that they broke the trees down. Even the most sluggish of the animals left their homes and fled away from the mountain.

After a time these disturbances ceased, and Bruin and his family wandered back up the mountain. But, somehow, things looked different. The trees and bushes were all dead, and the green meadows where the huckleberries used to grow were buried under a layer of soft ashes.

All at once they came out upon the edge of a great precipice. They could go no farther, for in front of them, where the mountain had risen so many thousands of feet, there was a hole nearly a mile deep and several miles across.

In the bottom there was a red-hot mass of lava, which bubbled up, and threw out great jets of steam.

What it all meant the bears did not know, but it seemed as if the mountain had been melted and fallen in. One look was sufficient, and then they turned and fled from the spot.

Year after year passed, but the bears did not return. The lake of lava at last became cold. The rains fell and gathered in this old crater of the sunken Mt. Mazama.

Explorers discovered this beautiful lake hidden away in the forests which now cover the summit of the Cascade Range. The surface of the lake lies two thousand feet below the top of the circling cliffs which formed the old crater.

The water is nearly half a mile deep, and clear and blue it lies there in the quiet of the mountain woods. On an island in the lake there is a small volcano, but it is also covered with trees. Probably it has been centuries since it threw out ashes and lava.

The eagles build their nests in the cliffs, and the deer come down to drink. Will it always be so? We cannot tell. Some time the fire may be lighted again, and smoke and ashes fill the sky, but we hope not.

This is the story of Mt. Mazama, the mountain which fell in. Do you wonder that it is not located in the geography?

———

BLACKBOARD WORDS.

Ranier (rā'nēr), **Willamette** (wĭl-ä'mŏt), **suffocating** (sŭf'fṓ-kā'ting), **disturbance** (dĭs-tŭrb'ans), **century** (sĕn'tū-ry), **sufficient** (sŭf-fĭsh'ent).

Jet = a sudden rush of water from a pipe.

Crater = the mouth of a volcano.

Huckleberries = the fruit of a low shrub.

THE LAVA PLATEAU OF THE NORTHWEST.

IF you want to get the juice out of an orange without peeling it, how is it done? Why, it is a very simple matter. Cut a little hole in the orange, and then squeeze it in your hands.

The great round earth on which we live is like an orange in some ways. It has a hard skin, or crust, on the outside, while it is soft on the inside.

Now, if there were a hole, or crack, in the crust of the earth, and some mighty giant should squeeze it, what do you suppose would happen? The soft material inside would come up through the cracks and run out over the surface exactly as the juice of an orange does.

Many different times in the history of the earth the melted rock inside of it has flowed out and over the green surface, making it rocky and barren. We must not think, however, that

REFERENCE TOPICS.
The crust of the earth.
The interior of the earth.
Locate the Columbia Plateau.
Origin of this plateau.
Columbia River canyon.

a giant really squeezed the earth, for there are no such things as giants. Instead of that, the lava was pressed out by the weight of the crust upon which we walk.

Our earth was once a fiery, glowing mass, like most of the stars, but now the outside has become solid and cold. At least, it seems solid, except when we feel it rocking during an earthquake.

Far below the surface it is still soft and hot. The crust is very heavy, and once in a while it settles down a little, and squeezes out some of this soft material, which we call lava.

You may wonder how we know that it is hot inside. In many parts of the earth lava can now be seen in the craters of volcanoes, steaming like some hot pudding. Many of the hot springs which are so abundant upon the Pacific Coast are caused by the heated rocks far below the surface. In some places mines have been worked that are nearly a mile deep. It has been found that the deeper the miners go the hotter it becomes. So we are quite sure that it is hot enough to melt the hardest substance not very many miles below the surface.

In portions of Oregon, Washington, and Idaho so much lava has been squeezed out that it has formed a high table land, or plateau, hundreds of miles in extent. It is called the Columbia Plateau, because the Columbia River flows across it.

The plateau was originally almost as level as a floor, but since the lava cooled, cracks have formed in it, and some portions have been raised to form high mountains.

How do you suppose this country looked before the lava flood buried it? It probably looked very much as mountains generally do. There must have been hills and valleys and running streams.

There came a time of terrific earthquakes. Great cracks formed in the rocks, and floods of fiery lava flowed up through them. The lava was very thin, and ran over the country, almost as easily as water would have done. It filled the valleys first, leaving the hills sticking up; but the heat must have been so great as to kill every living thing over many hundred square miles.

Then for many years no more lava came out. If we had lived there we should have felt safe again. The steaming lava became entirely cold. The winters and summers succeeded each other, until the hard rock crumbled a little on the surface, and trees grew up. Among them were pines and spruces, just like those we find on the mountains now. There must have been animals and birds also.

Then again, without warning, the crust was broken, and more lava came boiling out. It killed and buried the forests, and spread farther than it had before. After a time it was quiet again.

How many times this was repeated we hardly know, but at last the whole country, for hundreds of miles around, was completely buried.

These would have been terrifying sights if we could have seen them all. Steam, hot air, volcanic dust, and fiery lava were everywhere. It would have seemed as if the earth were turning inside out, and that everything upon it was to be killed.

Thus the Columbia plateau was made. After the lava had become cold, the rain water formed lakes at different spots upon its surface. Many interesting animals lived around these lakes. Their bones, which are still found, show that they were quite different from the animals living there now.

Far to the east of the lava plateau, were the Rocky Mountains. The lava had not covered them. The streams from these mountains flowed westward, and united in one large river, which we call the Columbia.

Ever since the Columbia began, it has been cutting its channel into the lava of the plateau. It has now the deepest and most rugged cañon of all the rivers of the Northwest.

The river has cut through the different layers of lava which flowed at different times. What we can see now in the cañons enables us to tell what happened so long ago.

We might compare this plateau to a layer-cake.

Each stream of lava would then represent one layer in the cake, and the soil between the layers the jelly. How boldly and clearly the layers of black lava stand out on the walls of the cañons. The thin layers of soil between them contain fragments of petrified trees and impressions of leaves. They tell the story of how the country was once buried by the lava.

BLACKBOARD WORDS.

Columbia (kö-lŭm' bĭ-a), fiery (fī'er-y, or fī'ry), glowing (glö'ing), petrified (pĕt'rĭ-fīd).

Glowing = white with heat.

Volcanic dust = fine particles of lava thrown out of a volcano.

Petrified trees = trees that have been turned to stone.

DOWN IN A GOLD MINE.

IF it were not for the gold hidden away in the mountains of the Pacific Coast, this region would not contain as many people as it does. In the early days, when gold was first discovered in California, there were no railroads.

When it was known that gold was to be had here for the digging, thousands of people started from the East for California. They had to encounter all kinds of dangers. They crossed the broad deserts, climbed mountains, in whose cañons Indians waited, or sailed half around the world.

After the pioneers reached California, they had yet to find just where the gold was. They explored the brooks and rivers of the Sierra Nevada Mountains, and discovered that in many places the

REFERENCE TOPICS.

Placer mining.
Quartz.
Quartz veins.
Gold.
Mother-lode.
How gold is mined.

"MAY LUNDY" GOLD MINE—NEAR THE SUMMIT OF THE SIERRA NEVADA MOUNTAINS.

gravels in their beds were full of grains of gold. This is placer gold, and digging for it is called placer mining.

The miners found little pieces of quartz with the gold, and soon discovered that both came from quartz veins, which appeared wherever the rain, or the streams, had washed the soil away from the rocks.

The little white pebbles, which we find in all the brooks, are quartz. They are so hard that your knife blade cannot scratch them, and often as clear and transparent as glass.

A quartz vein is a long, narrow band of quartz extending across the country. Quartz is so much harder than the other rocks that it often stands up in prominent points above the rest of the country.

All the children who live in the Sierra Nevada Mountains have heard of the Mother-lode. Those who live in other places would perhaps like to know something about it. The Mother-lode is formed by a line of quartz veins, which reach for more than a hundred miles through the foothills. These veins are very large and rich, and the miners called them the Mother-lode, because they thought the gold in the gravels of the streams all came from them.

Hundreds of mines have been worked here, and every one who is looking for a mine, wants it to be upon the Mother-lode, because he thinks it is so rich.

We must not think that all the quartz pebbles which we find in the brooks contain gold, for we would be greatly disappointed. The miner sometimes spends years hunting for a vein of quartz with enough gold in it to pay him for working it. He prospects the vein by pounding a piece of the quartz to dust in a mortar, and then washing away the dust in a pan, or spoon made of horn. If there is any gold, it settles to the bottom, and appears as a string of little shining yellow grains.

An old prospector had lived for years in a log cabin in a gulch in the mountains. He had a mining claim upon the Mother-lode, but for a long time had not been able to find just where Nature had put the gold, for she does not sprinkle it in all the quartz.

The day came at last when he found some quartz with specks and threads of gold. The disappointed look in his face was changed to a happy one. He built a new cabin, and threw away his old clothes.

He had worked years, digging holes along the vein of quartz, in the hunt for gold. These holes looked like so many wells, only there was no water in them. He had raised the quartz from the bottom of the holes by hand. The windlass which he used, with its rope and bucket, looked just like that employed by well-diggers.

Now, in place of this windlass, there stands a large mill, from which comes, through all the day and night, the steady thump, thump, of the heavy iron stamps, as they pound the quartz to pieces, and set free the shining grains of gold.

We will go down in the mine, and see what he has found. At one end of the room is a dark hole, surrounded by a railing. It is called a shaft, and through it the quartz is raised to the surface.

A steel rope is running up from the shaft, and over a wheel on some timbers above us. A little behind stands the engineer, ready to stop the machinery at a second's notice.

As we watch, a great square bucket, or skip, as the miners call it, comes in sight, rising out of the dark shaft. It passes to the floor above, where the ore is dumped, and is then lowered for us. We climb in, but not without some fear. At a signal, the engineer moves a lever, and we seem to fairly drop into the dark hole.

Down, down, we go for some moments. The air becomes cold, and by the light of the feeble candles we catch glimpses of mossy timbers, and bare, wet rock, as we fly past. Several lighted stations, where men are at work, come into view, and quickly disappear.

Little streams of water run down the sides of the

shaft, and drip upon us, but with rubber coats on, we do not mind it.

The bucket slackens its speed, and comes to a stop close to a platform, and we climb out. We are two thousand feet down in the earth, and although it is cold, the air is not bad, for there are pipes leading to the surface, through which fresh air is constantly pumped.

The men began digging upon the vein of quartz at the surface, and followed it all the way down this shaft. They think it extends much deeper still.

To the right and left of the landing upon which we stand, tunnels, or drifts, as they are also called, extend away into the darkness.

We start out to walk to the end of one of them, where the miners are at work breaking down the quartz. The timbers which hold up the roof of the tunnel hide the most of the vein, but in a few places we can see it glistening brightly.

We meet a group of men at the end of the tunnel, and stop to see what they are doing. Here stands an iron car, holding about a wagon load of the ore. It is pushed back and forth between the place where the men are at work and the shaft.

Two men are loading it with chunks of quartz, which have just been blasted down from the vein, which we see sparkling overhead. Another man holds a short steel bar, called a drill, while his companion strikes steady blows upon it. In this way a round hole is slowly cut in the solid rock. This is called drilling.

Holding a candle close to the vein, we can see little specks of gold scattered through the quartz. The foreman calls this rich ore, and we are ready to agree with him. A wagon load of it would make us almost rich.

It is nearly noon, and the men are going to blast down some more of the quartz, before going up to their dinner. Sticks of dynamite, which look like candles, only they are yellow, are placed in the holes which have been drilled. A dark, thick string, called a fuse, is put in the end of each, and left sticking out of the hole.

When all is ready, the fuse is lighted, and we hasten back through the tunnel, and enter a side-tunnel, or cross-cut. Here we are safe, and wait for the blasts to go off.

Suddenly, we hear a sharp click, seeming to come out of the wall of the tunnel. Then there follows an explosion, which shakes the solid rock.

It is very dangerous to work in some mines. If the rock is soft, it keeps settling slowly into the tunnels, breaking timbers more than a foot through. In some mines, there is so much water that the pumps have to be kept going all the time, or the men would be drowned.

The men who work in mines get so used to living underground that they do not think any more about it than we do of going into a dark cellar.

We hasten back through the smoke, which has come from the blasts, and reach the shaft. Our guide pulls a cord, which gives the engineer the signal, and we are drawn up again in the bucket.

BLACKBOARD WORDS.

Quartz (kwarts), **transparent** (trăns-pár′ent), **explosion** (ŏks-plŏ′zhŭn), **dynamite** (dĭ′ná-mĭt), **engineer** (ĕn′jĭ-nēr′), **machinery** (má-shēn′er-y), **lode** (lŏd).

Quartz = a hard, glassy mineral.

Prospect = to look over or explore for something.

Lode = a metallic vein, or series of veins.

Mortar = a strong vessel in which substances are pounded.

Stamp = a kind of heavy hammer for crushing ores to powder.

Windlass = a machine for raising weights.

Ore = the natural condition of a metal.

Shaft = a well-like excavation in the earth.

Drift = a passage cut through the rocks, a tunnel.

Dynamite = an explosive substance.

WHERE THE QUICKSILVER IS MADE.

WHO has not seen the silvery substance in the tube of a thermometer, and noticed how it rises when it grows warm and falls when the cold comes again; or, if the bulb be broken, followed with wondering eyes the glittering drops as they rolled over the floor?

This substance, so heavy and bright, which behaves so strangely, is quicksilver, or mercury. When people first discovered it they called it liquid silver, because it looked so much like silver. It is the only metal which looks like a liquid at the ordinary temperature, but there are many others which become liquid if they are put in a furnace where it is very hot.

Quicksilver is useful for many purposes. It is mixed with tin to form the coating for the backs of

REFERENCE TOPICS.

Different forms of quicksilver.
Where found.
Volcanoes.
Hot springs.
A quicksilver mine.
Extraction of quicksilver from the ore.

169

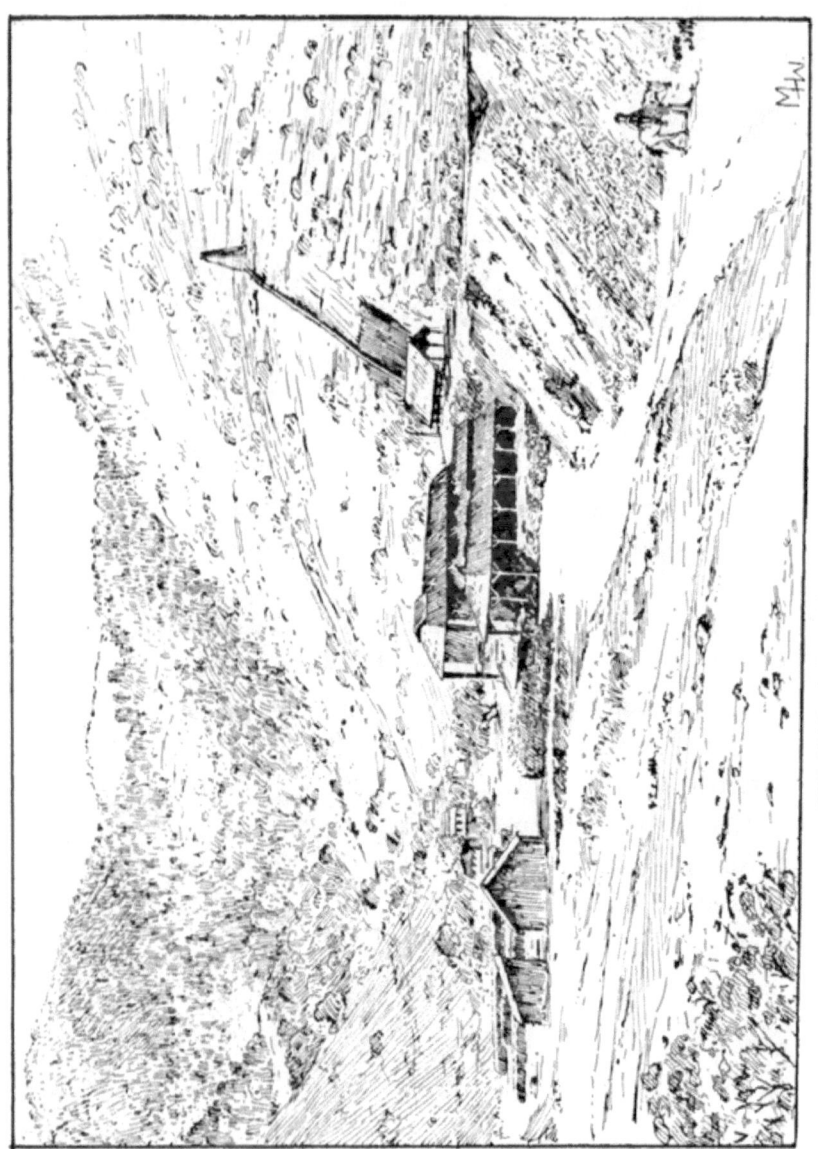

NEW IDRIA QUICKSILVER MINE, CALIFORNIA.

our mirrors. The miner uses it to collect the little particles of gold as the water carries them away. Calomel is one form of quicksilver. We may have some time taken this white powder as a medicine, and can remember how badly it made us feel.

Did you ever think that we do not get many things without working for them? The hunter has to tramp often many long miles before he finds any game. Our lessons, too, cannot be learned without hard work.

Nature treats us in the same way. She has hidden away her most precious things in the rocks, and we have to hunt long and earnestly for them. She does not give us quicksilver in the pure condition in which we see it in the thermometer, but combined with sulphur in the bright red mineral known as cinnabar.

The prospector spends his life hunting for minerals. He goes through all the mountains, and looks carefully at the many kinds of rock, and perhaps at last discovers some that contain little specks of this mineral about which we are talking, the bright red cinnabar.

Opposite the Sacramento Valley, near the summit of the Coast Ranges, there were once, many, many years ago, some great volcanoes. We all know that volcanoes are mountains out of which

come smoke and ashes, and sometimes fiery masses
of melted rock.

The volcanoes at last became cold, but the
springs about them remained hot for a long time.
Some are warm even at the present time, and are
used for bathing and drinking, as they contain substances which are valuable as medicine.

Where many of these springs run out over the
surface of the ground, prospectors have found deposits of cinnabar. The cinnabar was brought up
by the water from deep down in the earth, where it
is so hot that the rocks are almost melted.

In this region there is a little stream called Sulphur Creek, and along it, there are many hot
springs and veins of cinnabar. One large spring,
in particular, comes out of the ground on a hillside facing the creek, and here some miners have
dug a tunnel hundreds of feet long. We will take
advantage of their work to go under the ground, and
possibly we shall find something very interesting.

In the story books one goes on imaginary excur-
sions to the center of the earth, crawls through
caverns, and is let down over precipices to the edge
of boiling lakes, but here we are going to take a
real trip away under the ground, far from the
bright sunlight, and see with our own eyes what
Dame Nature, who seems never to get tired, is doing
there in her hidden workshop.

Hot, steaming water runs out of the tunnel, bringing with it a current of warm, choking air, which smells much as a lighted sulphur match. However, we need not be afraid, for the miners work here all day, although they have to come out of the tunnel once in a while for fresh air.

Before entering, we have to take off our outer clothes, for our guide, who is dressed very lightly, tells us, as the sweat pours down his face, that it is rather warm inside.

Holding a lighted candle in one hand, and in the other a little hammer to knock off specimens, we start in single file into the dark hole. On first getting inside we commence to cough, and are almost choked with the hot, stifling air, but after a time we get used to it, and manage to keep up with our guide.

We tramp on with our dim candles for some moments, passing now and then a narrow cavern, from which comes the sound of gurgling waters. At last we reach the point where the miners are at work, and we stop and look around. What wonders meet our eyes! Deep, narrow crevices lead away, until lost in the darkness, in which we imagine strange shapes, as out of them come the steam and choking vapors from the unknown regions below us.

We hear running waters in every direction.

They pour from some of the openings, almost boiling hot, and drip upon us from overhead. The walls everywhere sparkle in the light.

The hot waters are bringing up many other things besides the cinnabar, and are gradually filling up the open caverns with the most beautiful specimens. In addition to the bright red cinnabar, there is the yellow sulphur, and if we look closely, a little gold will be found in some places.

Most beautiful are the little crystals of sulphur which form from the choking vapors which we are breathing. They coat the walls, and sparkle like thousands of gems whichever way we turn.

The sweat covering our bodies, the stifling and poisonous air, the boiling water at our feet, and the sparkling walls, shutting us in on all sides, make it easy to imagine ourselves miles below the surface of the earth.

We can remain no longer, and hurry back to the fresh air of the outside world. We have had a strange trip into the earth. We have seen one of the most wonderful quicksilver mines in all the West. In most mines the water is cold, and Dame Nature is taking a rest after her work. She is waiting for new earthquakes, new volcanoes, and new hot springs.

Let us follow the ore from the mine and see what becomes of it. A little car running upon a wooden track brings it to the mouth of the tunnel. There it is put upon wagons and hauled to the mill, in the valley, where it is placed in a furnace, over a hot fire.

There it is roasted for a long time. The quicksilver is driven off in the form of invisible vapor, and passed into cool chambers, where it is condensed in the same way as the moisture from the air condenses upon a glass of cool water.

Working with quicksilver is very dangerous, for if one breathes much of the gas from the furnace, or the dust from the ore, it will slowly poison him. The Chinamen who are employed in most of the mines and about the furnaces go with moist cloths tied over their noses and mouths.

BLACKBOARD WORDS.

Thermometer (ther-mŏm'ĕ-ter), **calomel** (kăl'ō-mĕl), **mercury** (mer'kū-ry), **cinnabar** (sĭn'na-bär), **sulphur** (sŭl'fŭr), **glittering** (glĭt'ter-ing), **precipice** (prĕs'ĭ-pĭs), **crevice** (krĕv'ĭs), **ore** (ōr), **vein** (vān), **invisible** (ĭn-vĭzĭ'-b'l).

Mercury = a liquid metallic element.

Silver = a soft, white metal.

Thermometer = an instrument for measuring temperature.

Sulphur = an inflammable yellow mineral.

Mineral=an inorganic substance, having a definite composition.

Vein=a narrow mass o. ‿k intersecting other rock.

Tunnel=a passage cut through rocks at right angles to a vein.

Specimen=a sample; a small part of anything.

Crevice=a narrow opening resulting from a crack.

Vapor=any substance in a gaseous condition.

Ore=the native form of a mineral.

Condensed=made smaller, changed from a gas to a liquid.

Furnace=a place for melting metals.

THE AUTOBIOGRAPHY OF A NUGGET.

YOU must not expect me to tell just how I was made, or all the things that have happened to me. You would not understand it all.

Besides, I am a little puzzled myself to know who left me in the vein of quartz. However this may be, I lay for a long time deep down in the earth, with solid rock all about me.

It seemed for a time that I was to stay there forever, but as the years went past it began to be less dark, and I could see a little daylight coming down through the cracks in the rocks above.

The frost and the raindrops were at work with their picks and shovels, breaking the rocks apart and rolling the little grains down the mountain slopes to the brooks.

The brooks were tired of flowing so fast and

REFERENCE TOPICS.

Nuggets.
Veins.
How the rocks are broken down.
Story of Sierra Nevada Mountains.
Ancient river channels.
Hydraulic mining.

177

tumbling over the rough bowlders, and they were glad to help all they could in breaking the mountains in pieces. They picked up the grains of sand, and carried them along, but the pebbles and bowlders they could only roll over and over along the bottom.

They finally ground to pieces all the pebbles but those made of quartz. This interested me, because it was the quartz which held me so tightly.

At last the rock and quartz were broken away, and I rolled out upon the surface of the ground. How different everything seemed. Now I could enjoy life. I was upon a hill upon the western slope of the Sierra Nevada Mountains, but they were not as rugged and wild as they are now.

I had heard it whispered that there was a giant inside the earth, who slept the most of the time, but when he turned over he raised the mountains, and made them tremble. However that may be, it had been a long time since the mountains had been disturbed, and the frost and the raindrops and their assistants had almost torn them down.

They were still at work, and did not want me to lie there in their way. They were jealous of my pretty yellow color. They need not have bothered, however, for there were then no men there looking for nuggets like me.

As I lay upon the mountain side I saw some

strange animals feeding upon the bushes by the river. There was a rhinoceros, and a large camel with a hump on its back. Farther away there were other large animals, which looked like elephants. Long after, when I was brought down to San Francisco, I learned that they were mastodons.

The raindrops wanted to roll me into the brook. They washed the sand from under me, and let me go rolling down the bank. Finally, after a long time, I was tumbled into the river, and sank in a deep hole.

The river washed sand and pebbles over me. Sticks of wood and some large bones were mixed up with the sand. The bones must have belonged to one of the animals I had seen.

The river flowed over me for a long time, and buried me so deeply that I thought I would never get out again. I was not alone, however, for other nuggets were scattered through all the gravel near me. I felt proud, for I was the largest of them all.

All this time the raindrops were bringing the little pieces of rock to the streams, and the streams were carrying them away to the sea. The mountains, after a long time, became so low that it did not rain so much upon them. Then the rivers became smaller. Their work was nearly done.

At last something happened within the earth, and volcanoes were formed. They blew out steam and ashes and chunks of lava. There were lightnings and heavy showers. The falling water washed the mud and pieces of lava from the sides of the volcanoes and into the rivers. The rivers could not carry it all down to the Sacramento Valley, and so their channels were piled full.

As a result of all this, I was buried many feet deeper.

After that the earth about me became very cold, and I concluded that the river above me was frozen. The cold continued for a long time, and when it went away it rained a great deal, and the river rose and swept along noisily.

The lava bowlders and gravel which had been washed over me had by this time become cemented, so that the water could not carry it away. Then it went to work and washed out a new channel where the rock was softer. At this behavior of the river I lost all hope of ever getting out again.

For a long time the river kept digging its new channel deeper. It at last made a cañon more than one thousand feet deep, and I was left on what was now a high hill.

When the world had become ever so much older, and many more things had happened, some men came walking along on the ridge under which I lay buried. They had pans and a pick, and would here and there dig up some of the gravel and carry it to a little creek. There they carefully washed it, to see if there were any little particles of gold in it.

If that was what they were looking for, I could give them a great deal. But they could not see me hidden so far below. After they had prospected at different places on the hill, they found enough gold to satisfy them, and then went to work to run a stream of water over the gravel. They wanted to wash it away so as to get at the gold.

The men built a reservoir, and laid a pipe from it to the place where they wanted to wash the gravel. Then they made some long boxes, called sluices, with little cross bars in the bottom, to catch the gold when the water carried the gravel through the boxes.

When all was ready, they turned the water into the pipe. With what force it flew from the nozzle. It looked like a stream from a fire engine, only it was larger and much more powerful.

The men turned the stream against the bank of gravel, and it tore it down very fast. The gray bowlders were rolled around as though they were little pebbles. As fast as the water washed the gravel down, it was carried through the sluices where the gold was caught.

When they reached the bottom of the gravel they found what the miners call the bed-rock.

This is the rock over which the old stream flowed so long before. In the crevices of the bed-rock they found nuggets as large as walnuts, and felt very well satisfied.

What a surprise was in store for the miners who had worked so long. One day the stream of water washed the gravel from around me, and with a rush of the muddy water I rolled out of the gravel bank. How they rejoiced at the great yellow nugget.

I was so heavy that it was all one of them could do to carry me. After being admired for a long time I was put in a safe place. Every little while, however, they could not resist coming to look at me.

They said I was worth many thousands of dollars. I was taken down to San Francisco and placed in a window, but with heavy bars around me, to keep people from carrying me away.

This is my story. I had an interesting life. My end, however, was a sad one. I was sent to the mint and melted down, and made into many different pieces, which people carried around in their pockets

---

BLACKBOARD WORDS.

Cemented (sĕ-mĕnt'-ed), jealous (jĕl'ŭs), sluice (slŭs), reservoir (rĕz'er-vwôr'), rhinoceros (rī-nŏs'ĕ-rŏs).

Rhinoceros = a large thick-skinned animal.

Mastodon = an extinct kind of elephant.

Volcano = a mountain which throws out lava, ashes, etc.

Reservoir = a place where water is stored.

Cemented = united firmly.

Sluice = a long box, through which water runs.

Nozzle = a short, tapering joint at the end of a hose or pipe.

Nugget = a native lump of a precious metal.

COAL, GRAPHITE, DIAMOND.

AN we think of three things which are apparently so very unlike? The first is a piece of coal, which is burning brightly in the grate. The second is the black lead, or graphite, in my pencil. The third is a clear, sparkling diamond in my ring.

Although they seem to have nothing in common, yet they are all formed of the same substance. This substance is called carbon, and it came from the plants which lived upon the earth a long time ago.

Graphite and diamond are pure carbon. Coal is not pure, for it gives off a suffocating gas when it is burning, and leaves some ashes. Does it not seem strange that the diamond, which is the hardest of all minerals, and which shines with such a beautiful luster, is made of the same substance as the dirty black

REFERENCE TOPICS.

Origin of carbon.
Different forms of carbon.
Formation of coal.
Kinds of coal.
Graphite.
Origin of diamonds.
Where are diamonds found?

soot which comes from the coal, and lodges in the chimneys?

The graphite is black, like coal, but otherwise, it is quite different. It does not burn, if placed in the fire, and for this reason it is used for crucibles to melt other minerals in. It is soft and greasy, and besides being used for pencils, is valuable for lubricating machinery.

It will be interesting to know how each of these three minerals was made. We will study the coal first, because the others have been made from it.

We all know what swamps are. Perhaps, in trying to go through them, we have gotten into the brush, and have been scratched and tumbled into the water. In such places, the vegetation grows very thickly. The leaves, twigs, and trunks of the trees, when they fall, are partly buried in the mud and water, and so, when they decay, cannot dry up and blow away as they would in the open air. Year after year the dead vegetation accumulates, until a bed a number of feet thick is formed.

Now, if something should happen to the brook which flows through the swamp, and the water should become dammed up, the swamp would be turned into a lake, and the bushes and trees would be killed.

When the brook was high, mud and sand would be washed into the lake, and the old swamp would be deeply buried. This is the way in which the beds of coal originated. In some coal beds, miners have found the stumps of trees still standing where they grew, and impressions in the mud of pretty leaves and ferns.

After the vegetation in the swamp has been buried, it still takes a long time for it to be made into true coal. In some parts of the country, vegetation is now collecting in swampy places, which will some time make coal, if it is buried and preserved long enough.

The most of our coal beds were formed so long ago that we can have no real idea of the time. The surface of the earth was very different, and the fruit-bearing trees, and higher animals, as well as man, had not yet come upon the earth.

The climate of a large part of the earth must have been warm, and like that in the tropics at the present time. The ancient swamps, of which we are speaking, contained luxuriant growths of palms, tree-ferns, lepidodendrons, and many other plants.

After the swamps had lasted a long time, the earth's surface would sometimes sink, and permit them to be covered by mud and sand, either from a river or ocean. As the years passed, they would become so deeply buried and pressed upon by the earth over them, that the vegetable matter would change its appearance, and there would at last result a layer of black shining coal.

Years passed, and some new earthquake raised the beds of coal, and the layers of sand and clay, high in the air, until they formed mountains. When people came they discovered the seams of this black substance sticking out of the sides of the mountains, or in the cañons. They found that it would burn, and were made very happy, for in some parts of the earth there are few trees which can be used for fuel.

All they had to do to get the coal, which showed upon the mountain sides, was to dig it out; but in some places, Nature did not uncover it, and they had to sink shafts hundreds of feet deep in order to get what they wanted.

We cannot tell how much of the heat of the sun is stored in the coal beds. We know that it must be a very large amount, for the rays of the sun were necessary to make the plants grow from which the coal was made. Some people have called coal solidified sunlight. We are not sorry that Nature has preserved the vegetation of the swamps which were upon the earth so long ago. It is pleasant to think that she did it for our especial benefit, but it may be that she would have done it just the same if we had no use for it.

There are many different kinds of coal. That

which was made last is the poorest. It is called lignite, because it is nearest wood in its appearance.

Coal which is older, and contains more carbon, is called bituminous. The best coal is found in the rocks which have been heated and squeezed the most. This coal is called anthracite, and is almost pure carbon. The soot which coal leaves when it burns, is formed of little particles of carbon which were not burned.

Lignite and bituminous coal are both found upon the Pacific Coast. Nature has placed in the rocks of California, so many different kinds of minerals, that when it came to the coal she must have got tired, for there is not a great deal here. There were, probably, not many swampy places in this region for the coal-forming vegetation to grow in. Coal, in greater or less quantities, is found in nearly all parts of the world. The whalers have discovered it far north of the Arctic circle.

Now let us see what is the connection between coal and the black lead of our pencils. Black lead, or graphite, is formed from coal. When coal is heated far below the surface of the earth, where there is no air to permit it to burn, it is changed to graphite. Ice does not seem at all like water, although it is only water under a different form. Thus it is with graphite, which is the carbon of the pure anthracite coal under a different form.

Now we come to the diamond. It hardly seems possible that this sparkling gem is made of the same substance as graphite.

When the diamond is heated very hot it disappears in the form of invisible carbonic acid gas. This is the deadly gas which comes from coal when it is burning. Our breath, as it comes from our lungs, is also laden with this gas.

Like the graphite, the clear diamonds were made deep in the earth, where it is very hot. The carbon came up through the rocks as an invisible gas, and condensed in little cavities, thus forming the beautiful diamond crystals.

You can understand how this was done by placing a small pinch of sulphur in one end of a glass tube, and heating it. The sulphur will be driven away as invisible gas, and condense again in little crystals in the cool part of the tube.

Diamonds have been made artificially upon the sides of furnaces where there was very great heat. These diamonds are no larger than a pinhead, and are not fit for jewelry. Nature makes the crystals of diamond as large as a robin's egg. They have shining faces upon them, but have to be cut and polished before they show all their beauty.

The most of our diamonds come from Africa and Brazil. A few have been found in California in the gold-bearing gravels of the placer mines.

We sometimes hear people speak of California diamonds. They generally refer to clear little crystals of quartz, and not to real diamonds.

BLACKBOARD WORDS.

Suffocating (suf'fo-kā'ting), **lubricating** (lū'brĭ-kā'ting), **luxuriant** (lŭgz-ū'rĭ-ant), **bituminous** (bĭ-tū'mĭ-nŭs), **anthracite** (ăn'thrâ-sīt), **lepidodendron** (lĕp'ĭ-dō-dĕn'drŏn).

Carbon = one of the elementary substances.

Luster = the character of the light reflected from the surface of a mineral.

Crucible = a vessel in which minerals are placed to be melted.

Tree ferns = a fern having a tall trunk, with a cluster of fronds at the top.

Lepidodendron = a genus of fossil trees.

Shaft = a well-like excavation in the earth for raising ore.

Carbonic acid gas = a poisonous gas composed of oxygen and carbon.

Sulphur = a yellow, inflammable mineral.

Crystal = the regular form which a mineral substance takes when it solidifies.

Laden = loaded, burdened.

E have learned that the surface of the earth upon which we live is changing all the time. What was once the ocean bottom is now dry land, and some of the mountains which used to rise so high have been worn down until they are now but little above the level of the ocean.

Have the animals around us always remained as they are now, or have they, too, changed, as the years have passed by? There are many things which make us feel sure that they have changed very much indeed. The strange skeletons which are often dug up are not like those of any living animals.

All of the animals have their fathers, and grand-

REFERENCE TOPICS.

Animals change.
The world without life.
Life in the sea.
Extinct monsters.
Reptiles.
Birds.
Horses.

192

fathers, and great-grandfathers, just as we do. If the animals do not change, the bones which we find which belonged to their grandfathers, who lived ever so long ago, ought to be just like the bones of those living now. But the bones of those ancient animals are so different, we must believe that they have changed.

There were birds long ago, but they were different from our birds, which sing so sweetly on spring mornings. There were horses long ago, but they were not like the horses which pull our heavy wagons. There were reptiles, but they were not like the lizards which we see sunning themselves on the rocks.

The skeletons which are often found sticking out of the banks by the river, or when wells are being dug, tell us a true story of many of the animals which lived upon the earth a long time ago.

Let us try to form a picture of those old times, when everything was so different. If we should go back far enough, we should find the earth without any living thing upon it. For long, long years, the waves dashed against the bare rocks. The world was young then.

At last, some life appeared in the ocean. There were first, little animals so small we could hardly have seen them without a miscroscope. Then appeared the little mollusks, with their hard shells, the soft worms, the crabs, and the floating jelly-fish. But neither through all the ocean, nor upon the land, was there yet an animal with a backbone.

The world would then have been a dreary place for us. We could not have gone either fishing or hunting, and there were no fruits or berries. To be sure, there were several sorts of clams and mussels, but we would have grown tired of them.

The years rolled around then as they do now, and new animals appeared. There were fishes after a while, but they were queer fellows, and very different from any which we see in the markets. They were the first of the backboned animals.

While the fishes were multiplying in the ocean, a few small plants began to grow upon the land, and insects finally came to feed upon them.

As the years went on, some of the fishes got so they could live out of the water a part of the time. It was pretty awkward walking on the land with their fins, and so it came about that legs took the place of the fins. Their whole bodies changed, and so at last these animals, whose grandfathers were once fishes, came to look more like the alligators than anything else.

These animals changed more and more. Many made their homes on the land, but others continued to spend a part of their lives in the ocean. They were the fathers of some of the strangest animals that ever lived upon the earth. We could not imagine anything more terrifying, even in our wildest dreams, than some of the animals which now came to live here.

LEAPING DINOSAUR.

One clumsy animal, which had a length of eighty feet, walked about upon its hind legs as the kangaroo does. Its body was as large as a whale. Its long tail dragged upon the ground as it moved sluggishly along the beach, or through the swamp.

There were others of a very different shape, which were able to fly by the aid of great, bat-like wings. They were not birds at all, but flying reptiles. They were of such size that they could pounce upon and carry off all but the largest animals. What a scampering to cover there must have been among the animals, when one of these monsters came flying through the air, looking for his morning meal. Animals fought and ate each other in those days just as they do now.

I am afraid we would have had a sorry time if we had lived in those days. Between the great monsters that swam in the sea, and crept through the jungles, and those which flew overhead, we would have had to be on our guard all the time.

Later there appeared on the scene other forms, more like the true birds, but they were still very different from any which we meet now. One of these early grandfathers of our birds was about the size of a crow. It had large jaws, filled with teeth, like the reptiles. Its tail also was different from that of the present birds, being like that of a lizard, but covered with feathers, as was the rest of the body.

The sea, the land, an l the air, were full of these

strange animals. Some were of a peaceful disposi-
tion, but others fought among themselves, and
awakened the echoes with their loud cries.

Among the smaller animals was one the size of a
fox, but having much the
appearance of the tapir,
which now inhabits South
America. Would you be-
lieve it possible that this
little animal was one of
the early grandfathers of
our horse? This is really

EARLY ANCESTOR OF MODERN
HORSE.

the fact, for so many bones have been found that we
can trace the whole line of grandfathers down to
the present horse.

There were many interesting things about this
little horse that lived so long ago. Instead of
having one hoof on each foot, it had four toes on
the front feet and three on the hind ones.

As the years passed, the descendants of the little
horse slowly increased in size. At one time they
were as large as a sheep, later, about the size of a
donkey, until at last they looked like our horses.
Our savage forefathers caught some of these wild
horses which roamed over parts of Asia and
Europe, and tamed them for use.

The little horse used to live in America. His
bones have been found in Wyoming. His descend-

ants grew up here, and finally all died before the American Indians came. The old Mexicans had never seen horses, and when the men of Cortez came they thought the horse and rider formed one animal.

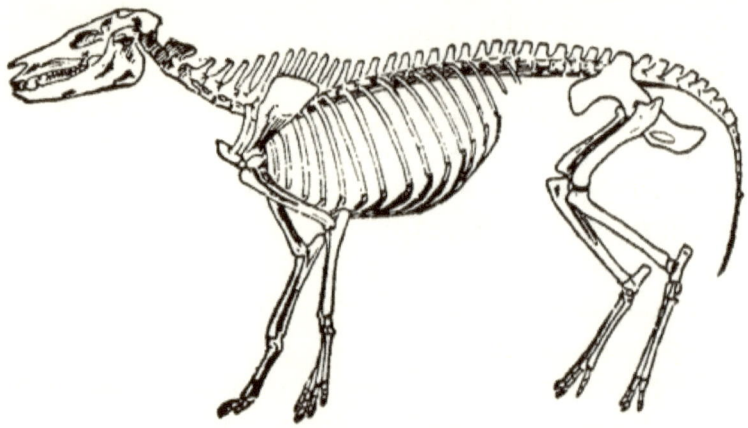

SKELETON OF THE EARLY ANCESTOR OF THE HORSE.

As the race of horses gradually became larger their toes disappeared, until now, as you all know, the horse has only one hoof on each foot. Above each fetlock there are, however, two little bones, or splints, which are remnants of the toes upon which the early grandfather walked.

While the years were passing, the great reptiles which we have learned about began to disappear. They seem to have been too clumsy to resist the fiercer animals which came.

Some of the lizards lost the use of their feet, and finally turned into the snakes which we all dislike so much. The python, of India, has still little remnants of legs under its skin.

The birds also changed. They lost their teeth and tails, and some of them looked much as our birds do. One kind grew large and heavy, and lost the power of flight. The ostrich has descended from such birds. It has powerful legs, and can run as fast as a horseman can ride. The ostrich still has wings, but there were others that entirely lost their wings. Bones of gigantic birds, without wings, have been found in New Zealand. They stood nearly ten feet high.

The great grandfathers of the fishes have always lived in the ocean, but those of the whales, seals, and porpoises used to live on the land. These animals, you know, are not fishes. They are mammals, have warm blood, and suckle their young.

The whale's great-grandfather then had four legs, and lived upon the land. But for some reason its descendants took to the ocean. Their bodies became fish-like in shape. Their hind legs entirely disappeared, and the fore ones were changed to flippers, to aid in swimming. Even now the whale cannot stay under the water all of the time, but has to come to the surface for air quite frequently.

Thus it is that the animals have changed through the long years that have passed since they came to live upon the earth. The body of each one changes to suit the demands of swimming, or walking, or flying.

The story of our animal friends is full of interest. When we know how they have changed, as well as how the hills and valleys are made, we have learned a great deal about our home.

———

BLACKBOARD WORDS.

Skeleton (skĕl'ō-tŭn), **microscope** (mī'krō-skōp, or mĭk'-rō-skōp), **mollusk** (mŏl'lŭsk), **reptile** (rĕp'tĭl), **kangaroo** (kăn ga-roo'), **al'ligator** (ăl'lĭ-gā'ter), **descendant** (dē-sĕnd'-ant), **disappear** (dĭs'ăp-pēr').

———

Mollusk = an animal of one of the grand divisions of the animal kingdom, generally with a hard shell.

Backbone = the column of bones in the back.

Fins = organs of a fish used in swimming.

Alligator = a large carnivorous reptile, found in America.

Kangaroo = a species of jumping marsupials.

Flippers = broad, flat limbs, used for swimming.

Splint = a thin piece of wood or bone.

www.ingramcontent.com/pod-product-compliance
Lightning Source LLC
Chambersburg PA
CBHW030542040726
47497CB00008B/2558